Most of the time, I can forget what Larry Fremont did to my family.

Most of the time, I can follow my mother's advice when she says, "Some things, Alicia, are best left buried." But tonight, it all came back to me. I aimed the remote at the television screen and cranked up the volume.

There had been a death. His personal accountant or lawyer, someone named Paul Ashton. Somehow I knew in my soul that Larry Fremont had killed that man. And if I would admit it to myself, I knew my insomnia, this locking of all my doors and windows, this habitual looking over my shoulder, went back twenty-five years to when I watched Larry Fremont throw my best friend off a bridge. And then laugh about it.

He had killed once and had gotten away with it. He has killed since. He would kill again. And I was terrified of him.

Books by Linda Hall

Love Inspired Suspense

Shadows in the Mirror
Shadows at the Window
Shadows on the River

LINDA HALL

When people ask award-winning author Linda Hall when it was that she got the "bug" for writing, she answers that she was probably in fact born with a pencil in her hand. Linda has always loved reading and would read far into the night, way past when she was supposed to turn her lights out. She still enjoys reading and probably reads a novel a week.

She also loved to write, and drove her childhood friends crazy wanting to spend summer afternoons making up group stories. She's carried that love into adulthood with twelve novels.

Linda has been married for thirty-five years to a wonderful and supportive husband who reads everything she writes and who is always her first editor. The Halls have two children and three grandchildren.

Growing up in New Jersey, her love of the ocean was nurtured during many trips to the shore. When she's not writing, she and her husband enjoy sailing the St. John River system and the coast of Maine in their 28-foot sailboat, *Gypsy Rover II.*

Linda loves to hear from her readers and can be contacted at Linda@writerhall.com. She invites her readers to her Web site, which includes her blog and pictures of her sailboat: http://writerhall.com.

Shadows on the River

LINDA HALL

Published by Steeple Hill Books™

STEEPLE HILL BOOKS

ISBN-13: 978-0-373-44336-9
ISBN-10: 0-373-44336-6

SHADOWS ON THE RIVER

This edition published by arrangement with Steeple Hill Books.

www.SteepleHill.com

Printed in U.S.A.

Then Peter came to Jesus and asked, Lord, how many times shall I forgive my brother when he sins against me? Up to seven times? Jesus answered, I tell you, not seven times, but seventy-seven times.
—*Matthew* 18:21–22

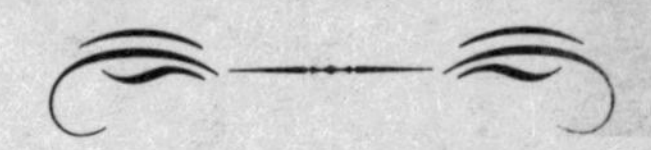

Acknowledgments

A special thank-you to Pamela Benoit Scott for all the information on ASL sign language and deafness and for great insights into the deaf culture.

A second thank-you goes to Jan Donovan-Downs for all of the information on childhood deafness.

PROLOGUE

Then Peter came to Jesus and asked, "Lord, how many times shall I forgive my brother when he sins against me? Up to seven times?" Jesus answered, "I tell you, not seven times, but seventy-seven times."

Matthew 18:21–22

The girl checked the time on her pink wristwatch and looked back at the front door of the school. Tracy, her best friend, should have been here by now. The girl sat down on the stone embankment and swung her legs hard, hitting the backs of her calves against the rock in a steady rhythm. No. She was wrong. Tracy wasn't her best friend. She used to be. Then Tracy got to be friends with the popular girls.

And then today happened.

"I have a secret to tell you," Tracy had whispered to her after lunch.

So surprised, all she could manage was a quick "Okay."

"I'll get my mother to pick us up. We'll go to my house and I'll tell you. I'll even show you my diary."

"Okay." The girl tried to keep the eagerness out of her voice.

"We can be friends again." Tracy had smiled at her, that big, broad smile of hers and the girl dared hope that they could go back to being the kind of friends they were in elementary school, best friends, sharing secrets, knowing everything about each other.

"Don't take the bus home. Just wait out front by the rock."

"Okay."

But Tracy hadn't shown up. It was late by now. All of the school buses had long since pulled out and she was alone in the front of the deserted school. It was hot and clammy and she was beginning to feel sick to her stomach.

From her perch on the rocks she watched two teachers leave, figures in the distance who didn't see her, the woman holding her skirt down against the warm breeze as she carried an armful of papers. She could hear them laugh from here. There were only two more days of school left before summer vacation and it looked as if the teachers were just as happy to be free as the students.

She looked back at the door. Maybe she should go inside and phone Tracy's house. She checked her wallet for dimes. But what if during the time she was inside making the call, Tracy's mother came?

So she waited.

A little while later she wondered if she should go into the school and see if anyone was still in the office. Maybe she should call her mother.

But her mother wasn't expecting her and probably wasn't even home. She'd phoned her mother at lunch to ask if she could go to Tracy's and her mother had seemed pleased. Even though she had never told her mother her problems with Tracy, her mother knew.

"You go," she had said on the phone. "Go and have a good time. I'll use the time to run some errands."

The girl spent the rest of the afternoon smiling. Tracy would soon be back in her life. And in a couple of weeks there would be church camp. With Tracy as her best friend again, it would be fun.

As she sat and sat in the blistering sun, her shirt stuck to her back in the heat, she finally came to the only conclusion she could—Tracy had played a trick on her. Tracy was probably at home with the popular girls and they were all laughing at her. She could imagine them, even now, sitting cross-legged on the wooden slats of Tracy's sundeck drinking lemonade and calling her a loser.

The girl jumped down from the embankment and felt a tear at the edge of an eye. Angrily she wiped it away. She looked down the empty street for a long time deciding whether to walk home. That meant about a mile along the hot road until the main part of town with its stores and the drugstore her father owned. She could stop there, she thought, and wait for him and get a ride home, but she'd have to hang around in the back until closing time. And that would be like forever.

No, what she would have to do would be to walk right through town, turn left for half a mile until she came to her street. She'd have to walk fast past Tracy's house. She didn't want to give her the satisfaction. She let out a sigh, shifted her book bag, and started walking, the black pavement hot through the bottom of her sneakers.

A quarter of a mile later she decided to take the shortcut. Maybe it would be cooler. She turned down the gravel road, which would become a dirt path winding past the church and through the graveyard beside it down to the river. Then it would be across the footbridge. A few steps later, she would be at the edge of her subdivision.

She wouldn't worry about that bridge. She knew what people said—that it was unsafe. She'd climb across the logs they put in the way and then hurry across it without looking down. A few minutes later she would be at her own house. She and Tracy had taken this way lots of times.

But it wasn't cooler on the path. If anything, it was hotter. She walked faster, a cloud of insects beside her. Perhaps when she got to the graveyard she could climb down the bank and get a drink of water from the river.

Her head felt hot, her legs heavy. She shifted her book bag. This wasn't such a great idea, she thought as she swatted away the bugs. Up ahead on the horizon was the church steeple. Good. Now it wasn't too far. A big drink of river water and she'd feel a whole lot better. Maybe her mother would even be at the church. Sometimes she went there for Bible studies and things. Or maybe somebody she knew would be there, Pastor Arnold, or the funny fat guy who mowed the lawns. Because the nearer she got to the footbridge, the more afraid she was feeling.

She began to run, and as she did she thought about Tracy. They hadn't spoken to each other in months. The notes she'd left in Tracy's locker were ignored and when she tried to phone her, Tracy was always not home. So why today? Did it have something to do with Larry Fremont? All of the popular girls were in love with him. Sure, he was sorta cute, but he was a lot older. Sixteen and Tracy was only thirteen, although Tracy was quick to point out that she would be turning fourteen in a month. Lots of fourteen-year-old girls go out with sixteen-year-old boys.

But there was something else she didn't like about Larry. That his family was the richest family in town, that they practically owned the town, had nothing to do with it. His mother owned the town's coal mine, which was where just about everyone's father she knew worked. No, it wasn't that. There was something about Larry that was just plain creepy. Maybe that's when she and Tracy stopped being friends, when she told Tracy what she thought of Larry.

She ran faster. She was running against the hot wind now, anger propelling her forward. She made her plans. This was the end of her trying to be friends with Tracy. Once she got home, she would act like she hadn't been waiting in front of the school for hours. She would pretend like nothing had happened.

If Tracy said something like, "Were you waiting a long time? We forgot all about you." Her answer would be, "Well, that makes two of us, because I completely forgot about going to your house. I got a ride home with my mom like always."

Angry tears coursed down her cheeks. How could she have been so stupid? How could she think Tracy really wanted to be her friend?

The path brought her behind the Fremont Mansion, and from that vantage point she could glimpse the blue ocean, frothy with whitecaps. A bit farther down this path and she would be at the church.

No cars were there. Maybe she could get in and cool off. She tried the doors. Locked.

Then she heard the voices, looked down toward the footbridge and saw them. Tracy and Larry. She put a hand to her mouth and slunk close to the side of the church. They hadn't seen her. Good.

She didn't quite know why, maybe it was something in their demeanor, but she decided to stay hidden. So this is why Tracy wasn't there to pick her up. She was with Larry!

She stole quietly to the graveyard where she hid behind a huge black gravestone under a pine tree. From here she could watch them.

They appeared to be arguing. She could hear their voices, high and loud, but not the words. At one point Larry placed his palm firmly on Tracy's chest as if to push her backward. She shouted something, flung his hand away and backed into the railing.

She wanted to call out, to warn Tracy that the railing wasn't safe. There were already parts of it that were broken, slats and boards that had fallen onto the rocks far below, but there she was, leaning against the railing with her whole weight. Larry put his hand on Tracy, only this time he was choking her.

The girl was about to call out. She didn't. For years afterward she would wonder if she could have somehow changed the outcome of everything in her future—her parents having to leave the church, her dad losing his business, her mother being ostracized—if she had only called out. Instead, she knelt in the hot buggy grass and put her head between her knees for a few moments and watched an ant crawl on her shoe while the voices on the bridge grew louder, angrier, more frantic.

She looked up again.

Larry was holding Tracy's shirt collar with both hands and glaring down at her. They were very close. Tracy was screaming, flailing. "Let me go! Let me go!" But he wouldn't.

The girl in the graveyard was about to rush forward and say, "Stop!" but at that moment, Larry let go of her. Tracy began to laugh as she backed seductively against the railing and put one foot up onto the cracked slat.

Larry was moving toward her now and when he got to her, he put his hand on her face.

At that moment something bit the girl's ankle. She looked down at it and scratched.

Tracy's screams caused her to look up and when she did, Tracy was tumbling off the footbridge, arms flailing, trying to grab for handholds in the air. Screaming. Screaming.

Larry looked down at her and laughed.

The girl in the graveyard leaned her head into the warm black gravestone and vomited onto the grass. Above her in the sun a gull called.

ONE

25 years later…

I turned over onto my side, pulled the quilt up around my ears and listened to the snowy wind rattle against the outside of my house. I snuggled down deeper into the warmth of my blanket. Still, sleep wouldn't come. I threw off the blankets and glanced at the alarm clock. 2:52 a.m. I sighed deeply, loudly and sat up on the side of the bed where I'd slept alone for eight years since my daughter, Maddy, was born. It was going to be one of those nights.

I rubbed the sleep out of my eyes and stuffed my feet into my slippers and switched on my bedside lamp. Beside me the novel I was reading lay opened and facedown.

It wasn't just the blizzard that was keeping me awake. Rod should have called today. We should have heard *something* one way or the other by now. This was stupid, I thought, yawning and tying my terry cloth robe around me. What could I do right now, anyway? I couldn't exactly phone him at three in the morning, could I? I walked out into the hall, as another wintry blast shook my little house. The storm was worsening, as predicted.

I gathered my hair up off my neck and tried to still my thoughts. This was insane. I was just nervous, that's all it was. This project that Rod and I had bid on was just that—another project. There would be more projects. At least, that's what I tried to tell myself. Never mind that this was the biggest contract to come down the pike in a long time.

I made my way across to Maddy's room to check on her. We both needed the money this project would provide. If I was lucky, the money might just be enough to pay off all my credit cards. There were always unforeseen expenses with Maddy, with her special needs, plus there were all the normal things she wanted, like a new pair of ice skates. New ones, she kept insisting. Not secondhand ones. If we got the project, brand-new ones would be no problem.

As the wind increased, rattling the panes, I also thought about Rod. He and his wife Jolene were expecting their first baby, a daughter, in just a few weeks. They, too, were relying on this money.

And then there was Mark Bishop—newly hired, specifically for this project. What would he do if we lost it? In the two weeks he and I had worked together, we'd gotten to know each other pretty well—enough to know that we clicked. We spoke the same language—boats and boat design. We'd had many long discussions about sailing in rough weather, racing in light winds and whether Kevlar was better than nylon for small, light wind boats.

But not about personal things. I knew very little about his private life. All I knew was that he wasn't married and that he had moved to Nova Scotia from Florida, where he'd worked at a marina. For all I knew, he could have a girlfriend stashed away somewhere, or even a fiancée. But it went both ways. He didn't know anything about me, either. I have a whole lot of secret places that no one can enter.

So, whenever I start getting lost in his eyes, and start imagining how wonderful it would be to sail around the world with him, I have to call myself back. Even so, Jolene had decided early on that Mark and I were perfect for each other. Sometimes she could be worse than a mother, trying to fix me up with every and any available bachelor.

Why was I driving myself crazy on a snowy night? Mark and I would be working together for a long time. The contract was "in the bag." Those had been Rod's exact words. Yet, why hadn't we gotten any word? We should've heard a week ago.

The smoke detector in the hall chirped briefly, which is what it does when the power surges. I glanced up at it. This was promising to be the biggest winter storm of the season.

"Got your flashlights and candles?" Mark had said to me as we left work that afternoon. The early evening clouds had hovered gray, low and leaden above us.

"I think I'm ready," I said.

"Hey, you want to grab a coffee somewhere?" he had asked. I was momentarily taken aback. In the two weeks we had known each other, he had never suggested that just he and I go out. It was always the three of us, Mark, Rod and me, sitting together at the coffee shop on the corner, talking about budgets, plans or how we would fulfill the contract in the time allotted. Was this a work thing or a date?

"I have to get home to my daughter," I said. "I want to get us settled before it snows."

He knew I had a daughter, but not anything about her or why it was I had to get home early. I didn't date much.

The few men I'd gone out with over the past eight years had run, not walked, away from me when they'd found out about my daughter.

"Well, then," he had said, nodding his head slightly toward me. If he'd been wearing a cap, he would have tipped it—it was that sort of gesture. "We'll see each other on Monday. Stay warm this weekend."

A huge Nor'easter, which had been making its way up the Atlantic coast for days now, was finally reaching us here in Halifax. I had already done all the requisite things; stocked up on flashlight batteries and candles and made sure all my doors and windows were tightly closed. I had also filled the bathtub and containers with water, plus we had plenty of food. One never knew.

Despite the wind tonight, despite the storm, my daughter Maddy was tucked into bed and sleeping soundly, her soft, stuffed yellow animal, Curly Duck, nestled in the crook of her neck. I watched her for a minute before I bent down and pushed a ringlet out of her face. So peaceful. How I longed for that sort of peace in my own life. I ran the back of my finger over the smoothness of her cheek. She flinched slightly, but didn't waken. I pulled the blankets up around her chin and bent down to give her a whisper of a kiss on her forehead.

I rose. For a few moments I leaned against the doorjamb and watched her sleep. She's the only good thing that came out of a one-year marriage to a philandering bum.

I crept downstairs, wiping the sleep more thoroughly out of my eyes. I sat down at my quasi-drafting table in my studio/office. It had started out as a dining room in another life, but now was firmly devoted to my boat designs. My eyes blurred when I looked down at the technical drawings for the boat I was designing. Absently, I rubbed an eyebrow with the end of my pencil.

I looked up and out toward the back of my house. It was too dark to see, but I could feel the wind, fingering its way through the cracks around my windows, snow firmly in its grip.

I checked my e-mail. Nothing yet from Rod. As if there would be. Hadn't I checked it a dozen times before I went to bed at eleven?

Rod and Jolene own Maritime Nautical. Boat builders hire him to design sail-to-keel ratios, rudder length and shape. Rod and I were classmates at Memorial University in Newfoundland and we both have degrees in marine engineering technology.

His wife, Jolene, has been my best friend since high school. She has a degree in Business Administration and runs the business end of the company.

When I went to Newfoundland to study marine design, she stayed in Prince Edward Island and went to university there. Halfway through my last year at Memorial, Jolene came up to visit me. As soon as she and Rod met, sparks flew, and they've been together ever since. They were married shortly after Maddy was born, and have been trying, almost from the beginning, to have a baby.

About ten years ago Rod, Sterling Roarke and I, all engineering classmates, decided we'd go into business for ourselves. I ended up marrying Sterling. Within a year I was pregnant and Sterling was running around. It was only after we divorced that I learned the extent of his affairs. He also ran the business into the ground by not getting proposals ready on time, promising things and not following through and lying to me and to Rod. Nine years ago, Rod, Jolene and I decided to let him go and strike out on our own. I was eight months pregnant at the time.

We moved the business to Halifax, despite my misgivings about living here. After Maddy was born, I knew I couldn't work full-time. I've been taking the odd contract here and there, working from home. And then, of course, there is my own little sailboat that I've been fine-tuning and tweaking forever. I rested my forehead in one hand as I studied my sketchbook.

The project I was so worried about on this stormy night was a biggie. It would mean going back to full-time work. This was my chance, and I was ready, really ready. Maddy was doing well these days—remarkably so. When Rod called me two weeks ago, I figured fate or God was handing me a gift. Maybe things were looking up for me, finally.

The contract was to design from the keel up, a twenty-foot day sailer/racer for one of the foremost boat builders in Maine. It had to be fast. It had to win races. I looked down at my preliminary sketches. If I shaved a bit off the front end of the keel... And then the worries nagged again. Could I do this? What if I fail? What if they hate my designs? Even though I'd tested it on a million computer programs, there was no guarantee. The best computer program cannot totally duplicate what a real body of water does.

And then there was Maddy to think about. What if Maddy needed help in school and I wasn't there? I was feeling a vague unease and I wasn't quite sure why. I glanced at the time readout on my computer. Three-ten. I really should go back upstairs and try to get some sleep.

I've had insomnia for as long as I can remember. It goes back at least to when Maddy was born and I realized that I would be raising her on my own. It intensified ten months later when I learned the extent of her disabilities. Maddy is profoundly deaf.

A blast of storm hit the side of my house. From the dining room there was a door to a large wooden sundeck, and the wind came at it with such a ferocity that it seemed personal. I hugged my arms around me while the drapes quivered. I could feel the storm from here.

I turned up the thermostat. Then I walked around the first floor of my small house, touching things as I passed them; my glass model boat, the newest sailing mystery from the library, a pair of Maddy's gloves, her stuffed teddy bear, the framed picture of my parents. I don't know why I was doing this pacing. Nerves, perhaps?

Then I sat down in front of my drawing, picked up the remote and aimed it at the little television I keep perched on a wobbly end table. Maybe there would be news about the storm. Or maybe the sound of it would keep me company on this uneasy, lonely night.

On the all-news channel, a weather announcer stood in front of a map of the east coast and indicated with a sweep of her hand, the track of the storm. It would gain in intensity throughout the night, she said, and peter out by late morning or early afternoon. Scrolling along the bottom of the TV screen in red were the words, *"Severe weather watch for all of Nova Scotia, Prince Edward Island and parts of New Brunswick. Stay tuned to local broadcasts for more information."*

Scrabbles of snow hit my glass windows and slithered down like ghostly spiders. The cups in my kitchen cupboard rattled slightly against each other. I rose and stood beside the window and looked out. Snow swirled sideways underneath the streetlights.

"Please, God," I found myself praying, "Watch over us." I chided myself for praying. A long time ago I gave up on God. Yet, at times like this, I pray.

The news channel switched to another item and

suddenly my attention jerked abruptly to the television screen. There I found myself looking into the face of the very person who had kept me looking over my shoulder all these years.

Larry Fremont.

Something like lead settled in my stomach. Larry Fremont is the reason I am no longer a Christian. Larry Fremont is the reason I gave up on prayer. I sat down at my table and watched the screen. Another gasp of wind made my house shudder.

One of the richest men in Halifax, Larry Fremont's name has been linked to more than a few shady dealings down through the years. My fingers trembled. It's not like I hadn't seen his face in the newspapers or on posters, billboards or TV before. He'd run for mayor of Halifax a while back. He didn't get elected—maybe the people were too smart. He was one of those rich entrepreneurs who manages always to be in the public eye. Just like his mother, I thought. Something deep inside me groaned and I felt a rising nausea.

I ran a hand through my hair and swallowed. Most of the time I can forget what Larry Fremont did to my family. Most of the time I can follow my father's advice to put it behind me. Or my mother's when she says, "Some things, Alicia, are best left buried." Most of the time I can do that, not turn over the slime-covered rocks of the past. But tonight, with the winter storm battering my home and my thoughts, it all came back to me in crystal clarity. I aimed the remote at the screen and cranked up the volume, wondering if it would wake up Maddy. If it's loud enough she can feel the vibrations through the floorboards.

Even though Larry and I lived in the same city now, we had never bumped into each other on the street, which was a blessing. Had I been crazy to move to the same city in which he lived? Sometimes I thought so.

One thing I had done was keep my married name. Maybe that gave me an edge of protection. Or maybe I was only fooling myself.

I kept my eye on the television. There had been a death. His personal accountant or lawyer, someone named Paul Ashton, had been found dead in his hotel room in Portland, Maine. It was believed that Ashton had a heart condition.

"I don't believe that for a minute," I said it out loud, shocking myself with that outburst.

Somehow I knew in my soul that Larry Fremont had killed that man. And I knew something else, too. If I would admit it to myself, my insomnia went farther back than to the birth of Maddy, or even learning that I would be raising a deaf child. No, this chronic, fearful insomnia, this locking of all my doors and windows, this habitual looking over my shoulder, the prayers I utter at odd times of the day even though I no longer believe in God, went back a full twenty-five years to when I watched Larry Fremont throw my best friend off a bridge. And then laugh about it.

He had killed once and had gotten away with it once. He has killed since. He would kill again. And I was terrified of him.

TWO

I woke with a groan the next morning with Maddy jumping on my bed and me and then pointing excitedly toward the window where it was still snowing, but more gently now. The fierce storm of the previous evening had spent itself out and all that was left were huge, lazy flakes wafting earthward. I had not gotten back to sleep until almost four. I had watched the news, hungry for more information about Larry Fremont and the death of his financial adviser, but there wasn't a lot.

Ashton and Fremont were down in Maine discussing trade opportunities when Ashton retired to his room early, complaining of a stomachache. The maid discovered his body in the morning. He had not called down to the front desk or to his wife. That was all. I had clicked through several more news channels but found nothing.

I'd finally fallen into a fitful sleep then only to be awakened in what seemed like mere minutes when Maddy came in, signing that it was snowing, and that the snow was all the way up to the windows.

"I don't think it's that high," I signed, and laughed. I signed and spoke at the same time. "Did you feel it? It was windy. The house shook."

She signed excitedly, asking if we could go out and play in the snow.

"Later," I signed. "We'll have to shovel the snow, especially if we want to go out and get you those skates I've been promising you."

My fears of last night were for now erased by the sunny dawn. All would be well. In a day or two my coffers would be overflowing with cold, hard cash and brand-new, name-brand skates would be no problem. And Larry Fremont? He was in the news all the time, anyway. How was this time any different?

"We can get new skates? Not old ones?" she signed.

"Yep, that's the plan." I pulled myself up out of my bed. Oh, yuck. Did I feel awful or what? I needed about four more hours of deep sleep.

"Are you ready for waffles?" I signed, and then yawned, fell back on my bed. "Maybe I should sleep first," I said.

But Maddy would have none of that. She jumped on me, and we giggled and tickled for a while. Then I got up and put on my robe, and Maddy went and stood on tiptoes at my window. She ran her hand over the inside of the pane where snow was piled on the outside. I looked at her skinny, bare legs and her blond curls still tangled from sleep and thought to myself that she was the most beautiful little girl in all the world. I would give my life to not have the same thing happen to her as happened to me when I was a young girl, not too much older than she was now.

I tapped her shoulder and she turned to me. "You need your slippers," I told her. "The floor is cold. Get your slippers and then we'll make waffles."

"Blueberry waffles?" she asked.

"Sure." And then I signed something and she smiled and came into my outstretched arms.

We have a sign between ourselves which really means, "Come here for a hug, pumpkin pie," which is my nickname for her because of her blond hair with its pumpkin-colored tints. She didn't like the sign for strawberry blond. She was the one who came up with "pumpkin." I added the "pie." I held her fiercely and was surprised at the tears that swam in my eyes. I'm so very proud of her. When you have a deaf child, the learning curve is steep. First, there were multiple visits to specialists, only to discover that with the kind of deafness she had, a cochlear implant was a crapshoot. It might work. It probably wouldn't. I learned that deaf children are often a year or so behind in their reading and literacy. I took a sign-language course for parents of deaf children and taught her signing from babyhood on.

I told her how much I loved her and how proud I was of her and how she was the best ice skater in the world and how as soon as the roads were cleared we'd go get new skates.

"Today?"

"I don't know about today. It depends on how soon they come and plow the roads. And when we can get shoveled out."

The two of us headed downstairs to make Saturday-morning waffles. Maddy went and stood in front of the picture window and gazed out at the snow. The morning sun peeked through the clouds. It was a white, wintry wasteland out there, a pale desert after a sandstorm. Sun on snow always brings a beauty, a whiteness to the inside of a house that isn't there in other seasons. The snowplows hadn't been by yet, so there was no delineation between the frontyard and road. One hearty soul was already out there attempting to clear his driveway with his snowblower, but it had gotten windy suddenly and from here it looked like the snow he was blowing was landing right back where it started.

Later when the wind died down, Maddy and I would bundle ourselves up and try to clean up the place with our shovels. The task looked daunting. Maybe my kind duplex neighbor Gus would snowblow my driveway when he cleared his own. He often did.

I pulled out the waffle iron from under my cupboard beside the stove and plugged it in to warm it up. I got out the eggs and flour and frozen blueberries and while I did so, I aimed the remote at the television to see if there was any news of the storm. Or of Larry Fremont. Especially Larry Fremont.

The news was the storm, of course, which had left an estimated twenty thousand Haligonians out of power. I felt fortunate that all we'd had were a couple of flickers. There was nothing about Larry Fremont, or the death of his associate.

Maddy, now clad in her favorite slippers and pink fleece housecoat, helped me measure flour into the mixing bowl, getting it all over her hands. She was signing happily about snow and skates and how much fun we'd have later, and could we make a snowman? And a snow fort? And could we have a snowball fight? And could her friend Miranda come over to play?

"Hey," I signed, "Don't talk so wildly, you're getting flour all over the place."

She giggled and wiped her fingers on her housecoat before she signed again. "Can Miranda come over?"

I nodded and signed that we could do all of those things, except, for perhaps, Miranda. "It will be hard to get anywhere today," I signed.

Miranda is her school friend and deaf like Maddy.

The news flipped to a new item. I listened with one ear while I finished up the waffle batter.

Maddy said, "Look." She said these words rather than signed them and I was really proud of her for talking. I followed her gaze to a man on cross-country skis who was walking a dog. It looked windswept and barren, like some scene out of *Nanook of the North.*

"Can we go skating like him?" she asked me.

I did a sort of made-up finger spelling sign for skiing, because this wasn't a word I thought she knew. The two of us, like every deaf family, have a lot of made-up signs, "family signs," they're called.

"Can we go skiing, then?"

I laughed and said we had no skis. I poured the batter onto the waffle iron, filling every crevice. She kept her eyes on the snow while the waffle sizzled.

When it was done, I opened it up and took out the waffle, cut it in two and placed it on our plates. I poured on thick maple syrup, the real stuff, and we sat down and began to dig in. As we did so it struck me, as it sometimes does, that we didn't offer any kind of table grace. The only time we ever do is when my parents come for a visit. I grew up in the church with grace at every meal and summer church camp and memorizing Bible verses and Sunday School. There are times when I wonder if Maddy might be missing out.

She was pouring on way too much syrup and I signed that that was enough. She turned away from me, pretending not to see. That's what she does when she doesn't want to talk to me, she'll either turn her face away or close her eyes, scrunching them up and facing me defiantly. Although I love her to death, my little daughter can be stubborn at times.

I heard the name Fremont from the television and

turned quickly away from Maddy and aimed the remote to turn up the volume. But it was the identical broadcast that I'd heard before. No new information. What was I expecting? And why did I care so much anyway?

After breakfast Maddy and I spent a lazy morning cleaning the house and doing laundry and making a batch of ginger molasses cookies. Later on she "chatted" with Miranda via her computer and then watched TV. Other mothers mind when their children spend too much time on the computer, but not me. It enhances Maddy's reading. I tried to keep my eyes open while I sat at the table and worked a bit more on the boat design, but I was tired, very tired. What I wouldn't give for a nap.

The snowplow eventually came by, leaving a tanker-load full of snow at the end of my driveway. By early afternoon, I began to hear the sound of snowblowers in the neighborhood. If you closed your eyes you could almost pretend it was summer and these were lawn mowers.

Midafternoon my neighbor began snowblowing my driveway. I waved to him from the picture window. Bless him. My neighbor Gus and his wife, Dolores, often make sure my driveway is plowed. I rarely even have to mow my own lawn in the summer. I know they feel sorry for me, a single mother with a deaf daughter.

I looked again. There were two men out there working on my driveway. Gus was behind the snowblower and someone else wielded a shovel at the end of it. I peered more closely. Mark? Could that possibly be Mark? I squinted. Yes! Farther down the street was his car. I put a hand to my face. Why on earth was he here shoveling my driveway? And how had he driven these roads in the first place?

I grabbed my coat and pulled on my boots and signed

to Maddy to "Wait here. Watch from the window. I'll be right back."

I stomped through thigh-high snow to where Gus had cleaned a foot-wide swath to the end of my driveway. Mark looked up, saw me, grinned and put down the shovel and leaned on it rakishly. Mark has these studious, smart, good looks that can stop women in their tracks. With his neatly cut short, light hair, and his little rectangular glasses, he looks upscale; rich even, like he belongs in New York, not Halifax. No matter what he wears, clothes look so good on him. Like today. Even though he had pulled a ratty-looking, gray woolen toque down over his ears and that old man's green down jacket.

I called to him. "What are you doing here?"

"I thought you might need a plow out."

"And you came all the way over here?" The moment I said it, I realized I had no clue where he lived. He could live on the next street for all I knew.

"Actually," he said scooping another shovelful of snow. "I was up late. I got going on the interior design of the boat. I wanted to run some of these plans by you."

"And so you come out on a day like today?" Without calling first? I wanted to add.

"Why not?" He grinned a crooked little grin and I felt myself melting under his gaze.

"How did you even know where I live?" I was still astounded that he was actually here.

"Your address is on a lot of stuff at the office. It was easy to look it up online." He searched for my address? Stop it, I told myself, stop staring at him so intently.

I looked at the window and Maddy waved at me. I pointed. "My daughter. I have to go inside. But we'll be back. She wants to come out into the snow."

"She's signaling to you rather vigorously."

"She's not signaling," I said. "She's signing. She's deaf."

"Oh."

Inside, I helped my extremely eager and bright-eyed daughter into her snowsuit, wool hat and mittens. I did the same for myself, changing out of my grungy baking sweatshirt and into a nice sweater. Then I bundled up against the cold. The wind out there was still gusty.

Maddy rushed ahead of me out the door, arms spread wide. She immediately jumped into three feet of snow and giggled.

"That's my daughter, Madison," I told Mark. "As you can see, she hates winter."

"Just like me," he said while he pulled the gray cap more firmly down over his ears. "I was in Florida for three years. Some may call me crazy, but I really missed the winter. Had to come back home."

I looked at him. "This is home?"

We were standing on the sidewalk where he had started to shovel, while in the driveway Gus was still making passes up and down through the deep snow.

"Yep. Nova Scotia born and bred."

"Where?" I asked.

"Sydney."

"Wow. I grew up not far from there." When I told him where, a shadow seemed to pass across his face. Or was I just imagining it? My thoughts were interrupted, in any case, by Maddy.

"Look!" she shouted out loud.

"She's full of spunk," he said. "Must get that from her mother."

"I don't know about that. Today I feel totally out of it. I didn't sleep well last night… Maddy!" I signed when she looked over at me. "Come meet my friend."

She rose from where she'd buried herself and waddled over, completely covered in the fluffy white stuff. Mark bent down to her level and said very plainly, "Hello, Madison."

"His name is Mark. He's my friend from work," I signed to her. She smiled and said in her best voice. "Hello."

"It's nice to meet you, Madison," he said.

I interpreted and she signed, "It's nice to meet you, too."

"Do you like the snow?" he asked.

Through my interpretation they carried on a conversation for a few more minutes and at the end of it I marveled at Mark's persistence. My daughter made most of the men I dated nervous and ill at ease. And here was Mark, down at her level, making eye contact and asking her about school and her favorite things.

For the next hour the four of us cleaned the driveway and sidewalk. Even Maddy helped with her little shovel. After it was over I invited them all in, including Gus and Dolores, for hot chocolate and ginger molasses cookies.

When we'd all gotten inside and shed our sweaters, jackets, mitts and toques, I made a huge pot of hot chocolate in my grandmother's stockpot. I made it the old-fashioned way, with real cocoa and milk, the way we did in the little town on Cape Breton Island where I grew up.

All we needed were Christmas carols and a fireplace to round out the afternoon, but because Christmas had passed a month ago, we had to satisfy ourselves with just hot chocolate and snow.

"You have a nice house," Mark said looking around.

"Thank you," I said. "I like it."

Maddy and I live in a three-story town house. It sounds big because there are so many floors, but it's a skinny little place. If you put it all out end-to-end, you wouldn't end up with much square footage. The basement is basically a laundry room with enough space to store our bicycles and a few boxes. The main floor is kitchen, dining room and small living room. The third floor contains two bedrooms, Maddy's and mine.

Dolores, who knows a few signs, talked with Maddy while Gus and Mark and I chitchatted about the boat-building industry. Gus, a retired captain, used to captain the ferry that ran between Nova Scotia and Prince Edward Island a long time ago, before the Confederation Bridge was constructed.

After we'd each had a couple more cups of hot chocolate and had pretty well finished the batch of cookies Maddy and I had baked that morning, Gus and Dolores took their leave. But Mark showed no signs of asking for his coat. Maybe he really had come over to talk about the boat plans. I showed him what I had been working on in the middle of the night, while Maddy settled herself in the living room and turned on the television.

It was a matter of minutes before I realized that Maddy was watching the all-news station, not her usual fare. It was Mark who noticed why.

"Looks like she had a busy day," he said.

She had crawled up onto the couch and was fast asleep. I went and put a quilt on top of her. Before I was able to aim the remote at the TV to shut it off, the Fremont story was on. I stood, watching it for a few seconds.

Mark was standing in the doorway when he said, "I know that guy."

I jerked my head up at him. "Larry Fremont? You know Larry Fremont?" I was shocked.

"Paul Ashton. The man who died. I know him."

"Really?" I was incredulous.

He nodded, leaned his trim body against the doorjamb. "Our families know each other. The Ashtons go to the same church that I do."

"Seriously?"

"Yes, we know him."

"No, I meant, seriously you go to church?"

"I do. You?"

I shook my head.

"I used to. Not anymore."

"How are the Ashtons?" I asked.

"I just came from there. My parents have been with the family since this happened. Paul was a good man. Our entire church is feeling his loss."

I kept my voice even. "So this must be quite shocking to everyone, his dying of a heart attack."

Mark frowned, rubbed his chin. "That's the funny thing about it. No one knew he had a heart condition, least of all his wife."

We were standing and facing each other in the doorway. I said, "The news said he had an existing heart condition."

Mark shook his head. "No one knows why the media came out with that, but then again, I suppose the media has been known to fabricate things from time to time." He took off his skinny glasses and cleaned them on his shirt. The news had shifted back to the storm.

I aimed the remote and flicked the television off. Do I tell Mark that I know Larry Fremont? That we grew up in the same small town? I trembled a bit as I returned to the dining room where Mark was still leaning there and regarding me curiously.

"Are you okay, Ally?" There was concern on his face. "Is something wrong?"

"Nothing," I said. "I'm okay," I lied. "Just really tired."

THREE

By Sunday, the magic of the snow had gone. It was now dirty and a nuisance and piled where it shouldn't be, hindering the smooth flow of shopping and traffic. It was Sunday and we didn't go to church. Funny that I thought about that fact on this morning. Sundays come and go in our house and I never consider church at all. I guess it was having Larry Fremont on the news. Or having Mark in my house the previous day. Or learning that Paul Ashton went to Mark's church. Or even learning that Mark went to church in the first place.

I'd long ago spurned church when the one we attended had spurned my family. When all those long years ago they'd swept what had happened under the carpet, claiming I was the crazy one, that I had not seen what I knew I had. I never went back. The Fremont family were just too strong, too rich, too powerful. And our family wasn't. We didn't stay and fight. We left.

On this Sunday two things happened that changed everything for me. And by the time the day was over, I would realize that I should have listened to that uneasy voice the other night, the one that said nothing good will come your way, and that Larry Fremont is a murderer.

First, I was partially vindicated. The all-news station that I'd basically had on 24-7 since I first heard about Larry Fremont, came out with the truth. Paul Ashton had hit his head on the edge of the coffee table in the hotel room. They were looking into the possibility, still, that the fall may have been a result of a heart attack or brain aneurysm, but it was definitely a blow to the head that killed him. The hotel coffee table had been taken in for evidence. But I knew the truth. I was sure that Larry Fremont had hit him over the head with a blunt object and made it look as if he'd fallen into the coffee table. I would stake my life on this.

While I was watching it, the news cut away to Larry Fremont. I stopped and shushed Maddy, who was signing to me rapidly from where she was sitting on the couch. Larry Fremont saying how sad was this unfortunate accident and if the hotel was culpable in any way, they would get to the bottom of it. "Paul Ashton was a fine man," Fremont was saying into the camera, "and I was proud to have him on my team, even if for such a short time, and to work with such an upstanding individual." I'll give Larry credit, he looked near tears.

The reporter added that foul play had not been ruled out. I sat and watched the whole thing without moving.

On the couch, Maddy was dressed and signing, "When are we going to get skates?"

"Soon," I said. Fact was, I needed to get caught up with a few e-mails and do a bit of work first.

I went back to my computer and while I should've been working on the boat design, and particularly the rudder, which I was having trouble with, I was thinking about Larry Fremont and Paul Ashton. Money, of course. If Ashton was Fremont's financial adviser, and a Christian at that, you can bet he found some discrepancies in the books. I knew I would be proved correct. It would just be a matter of time.

It occurred to me that I could ask Mark about this. He might know something. Truth was, after he told me he knew Ashton, I'd become wary. I don't know why. Not many people knew about the Larry Fremont episode of my life. Even my parents don't even know the entire thing. Jolene does. I'd told her the whole thing back when we were in high school.

It'd taken me a while to open up to her. I had arrived at the high school on Prince Edward Island, a sad, scared girl from a little town in Nova Scotia, hurt and grieving and afraid of getting close to anyone. Jolene introduced me to sailing. Her family had a couple of little sunfish sailboats that we used to take out onto the Northumberland Strait in the summer. It was on one of these trips that I had told her my story, swearing her to secrecy.

I grew to love sailing. Gliding fast through the fierce waves was the only time I felt alive. I was in my own world out there, and when I could control nothing else in my life, I could control my boat.

I opened a few online newspaper articles, but couldn't find anything additional on Paul Ashton's death. By all accounts, he looked to have tripped on the edge of the hotel carpet and hit his head on the coffee table. I needed to dig deeper.

Because I didn't want to risk losing this information, I printed what I found. I ended up with quite a little stack beside my computer.

I got so engrossed in this work that for several seconds I didn't notice Maddy standing there beside me. Finally she tugged on my sleeve. "Mom, when are we going to get skates?"

"Just a few more minutes," I signed. "And then we'll go. And we'll even stop for ice cream on the way home. Would you like that?"

She signed "yummy" by rubbing her tummy and smacking her lips—a family sign.

"I like Mark," Maddy signed to me suddenly.

I looked at her. What brought that on?

"Really?" I said.

"He's nice," she signed.

"I'm glad you think so," I said.

"It was fun yesterday," she added, and I agreed. What was happening to me? I couldn't afford to fall for a guy like Mark.

We were getting ready to leave when the phone rang and the second life-changing event happened.

It was Rod. He sounded breathless. But more than that, he was angry. And the always even-tempered Rod I know doesn't get angry.

"Ally. Ally. You sitting down?"

"Yes, Rod, Rod," I said repeating his name the way he had repeated mine. "I am sitting here at my computer."

A pause.

And then suddenly I was concerned. "Rod," I said. "What's wrong?" Was something wrong with Jolene? Had something gone wrong with the pregnancy? They had been trying for so long. "Is everything okay?"

"Ally, brace yourself. We lost the project."

"What?" At first I thought he said baby, that they had lost the baby. It took me a moment to realize that the word he had said was *project.*

"The project. We lost it," he said.

"What are you talking about?"

"With Maine Boatbuilding. They gave it to someone else, get this, a bigger firm in California. California!

How convenient is that? They wanted a firm with more *resources.*" He sputtered out the last word.

I gripped the phone with both hands. Maddy was beside me on the floor, playing with two of her toy ponies.

"Rod?" I said. "How could this happen? We already gave them the general design. Didn't they *say* it was ours?"

"Yes, they did. They gave me every indication."

"I don't understand." I put my hand to my head, looked away from my blue-eyed daughter who was tugging at my sleeve.

"They found a firm with more people, their bid came in under ours. I've been on the phone for the past hour."

"You found this out today? On a Sunday?"

"I called Lew. At home. I was sick and tired of them not answering our calls. We should have heard a week ago. Two weeks ago, even. I thought, he's got to be home on Sunday morning. So I called him. I said, 'You owe us, Lew, what's going on? Why haven't we heard?' And that's when he told me."

"I absolutely can't believe it, Rod. We've done work for them before. Plus, we even hired Mark."

"I know. And they always *liked* our work. Lew did say they loved your design," he added. His voice trailed off and I knew what he was thinking. The project was major. It would have put us into the big leagues. Not to mention it would have paid a few bills.

"The whole thing stinks," he said.

"We have no recourse?"

"They were pretty firm on it."

"We should protest. Maybe we have a case." I put my hand to my head because suddenly all I could think about was the fact that I had not seen a cent of child support since early fall.

"There's nothing we can do about it. We can't sue. We have no legal grounds. The bids were fair and square and Maritime Nautical just lost out. That's the way it would play out with a lawyer."

I sighed. "Great." The two of us didn't say anything for a while.

"Ally, I know this affects you, but I've been thinking about you. I'd like you back on board. I'd like the three of us to be Maritime Nautical again."

"But you don't have enough work."

"I've been checking on a lot of stuff. There are a bunch of contracts we can bid on."

I asked, "What about Mark?"

"We'll have to let him go. I'm sure he wouldn't want to stay, not with his credentials and talent."

Why did the thought of not seeing Mark on a regular basis fill me with such sadness? I still could not quite believe it.

"Maybe we should meet this afternoon. I'd like to talk to Mark face-to-face. Jolene and I could come there, or you could come here."

I said, "Why don't you come over here? With Maddy, it would be easier for me."

Rod said, "That's what I figured. I'll call Mark. See if he's available."

I felt my chest collapse. Finally I said, "He was just here yesterday. We went over plans for the interior."

"Swell," he said drily.

"How's Jolene taking it?"

"I haven't told her yet."

"What do you mean you haven't told her?"

"She's out looking at baby furniture with her mother."

"This doubly stinks," I said.

"Ally?"

"Yeah?"

"I'm really sorry."

"It's not your fault."

And when we hung up, Maddy came to me and I told her that we couldn't go shopping for a while. I signed, "I have a very important meeting this afternoon here at the house. Rod and Jolene are coming over. And Mark, too." And because we didn't have an agreed-upon family sign for his name, I finger spelled it for her.

Immediately she grinned and placed the thumb and forefinger of each hand together at eye level, indicating that he wore glasses. She screwed up her mouth in the way that he smiled. Forever on, this would be our sign for him.

And then she paused, seemed to think and signed quickly, "It's okay, we can get skates tomorrow."

"Come here, pumpkin pie." She did. And as I held my daughter, smelled the little-girl smell of her hair, I wondered how I was going to tell her that there would probably not be any new skates for a while.

When I backed away from her, I signed. "Maybe tomorrow we can go and have a look at Value Village for some skates."

She immediately dropped her hands to her sides and stared at me. Then, frowning, she signed rapidly, "But you said new skates. New skates. New skates. New skates." She kept repeating this last part, her fingers becoming wilder, stiffer with each repetition.

"I know, pumpkin pie, but sometimes things happen. And Value Village has good stuff. We go there a lot."

She regarded me for a while without saying anything.

"A bad thing happened with my work," I tried to explain.

"I know," she signed without looking at me. "I heard you on the phone."

I stared at her. Sometimes I'm astounded at how astute she is. She's learned a fair bit of lip reading, plus she's always been able to pick up on my moods.

"It's not fair," she said.

"I know," I said. But by now my little daughter had shut her eyes tightly, turned her head away fiercely. When I tapped her shoulder, she held this pose. When I reached for her and stroked her hair, she jerked away.

Several times before my guests arrived, I went up to Maddy's room, but as soon as she saw me enter, she would shut her eyes and scrunch up her face.

Downstairs, I cleaned up our lunch dishes and loaded the dishwasher. I got out the coffeepot. Maybe people would like coffee. Why did it ever occur to me that things would work in my favor? Why did I even bother trying?

I thought about Maritime Nautical and wondered if it was time to quit trying to survive on this freelance stuff and get a real job, like with a corporation, or a big company. I've got both a BA and an MA in Naval Architecture and Ocean Engineering and I could be making a lot more money somewhere else. People with my kind of degrees are pulling in six figures at huge boatbuilding companies.

I slumped into my couch and got out the *Halifax Chronicle* and scanned the want ads. Not finding anything of interest in the *Chronicle,* I got up. Tomorrow I'd try to find a Saturday *Globe and Mail.* There are always more job ads in that paper. But there was one good reason why I wasn't farther in my career, and that was Maddy. And for one awful minute I resented her. She was upstairs not speaking to me because I couldn't afford new skates for her, and she was the reason I couldn't make more money.

But that awful moment passed in an instant.

Just before Rod and Jolene were due to arrive I went up to her room one last time. She looked up from her ponies this time and signed, "Can I go to Miranda's today?" Her mood seemed somewhat improved.

"I can't drive you," I said. "I have a meeting. And I don't know if it's okay with Miranda's mother."

"Can you phone her?"

I got on the floor and sat beside her. "How about if I call her when I go downstairs and see if Miranda would like to come over tomorrow. I'll pick you guys up after school," I said.

"Okay."

I ran my fingers through her strawberry curls, untangling them. I signed, "What would you and Miranda like to do tomorrow?"

"Get new skates."

"I don't know about that." But maybe I would rethink it. What was forty more dollars on my credit card?

I hugged her tightly for a few minutes before I went downstairs to call Miranda's mother, Katie.

"I'll pick her up," I offered, after making the girls' playdate.

"Great. Miranda will love that. Hey, did you get the notice about the deaf luncheon next month? It's a fund-raiser."

"Maybe. I think it came across my e-mail." I closed my eyes. I may have deleted it.

Katie said, "But you've got that new job, right? So, you probably won't be able to be involved? We'd love to have you come. How's the job going?"

"Well, actually…" I paused, caught my breath. "Maybe I'll come. Mark us down."

Katie and I were friends. Our daughters were the

same age and both deaf. They had been placed in the same regular classroom, where a full-time interpreter worked with them throughout the day. Katie was an extremely energetic woman who worked hard to help her daughter succeed. We had a lot in common, yet nothing in common. Katie didn't work. She didn't have to. Her husband's job provided all the money they needed and then some. Katie devoted her life to the deaf community, making sure that Miranda had the best possible care and opportunities.

I was grateful to Katie for all the work she did on behalf of the deaf community. Sometimes I felt I didn't have the time, strength or money to advocate for my daughter's care the way Katie did. There are times when I feel so overwhelmed.

Katie and her husband also had another child, a hearing girl who was four. Plus, they went to church. I'm not sure which one. When they would ask me if Maddy could attend with them, I always said no, even though Maddy sometimes begged to go and they had a full-time sign-language interpreter on staff.

They never pressed. I was grateful for that. Katie knew nothing about where I came from and what had happened to me, and why I was so adamantly against church. She probably figured I'd been raised like most of the people my age, in a secular family. It would probably surprise her to know I knew a few Sunday School songs. They popped into my thoughts at the oddest moments, as did prayers.

Rod and Jolene arrived ten minutes later. Jolene hugged me. She was looking more and more radiant. The fringed ends of a skinny, shimmery scarf wound many times around her neck, draped down across her round belly. She also wore a set of long silver chandelier earrings. I asked, "And how are we feeling?"

"Both of us are healthy and happy and waiting for this little girl to show her face. Only a couple more weeks."

I said, "Wow! I can't believe it's so soon." I paused. "I thought you were shopping with your mother today."

"Rod called me on my cell. He told me everything on the way over." She smiled widely and said, "All I can say is this is probably a blessing in disguise."

"How can you say that?"

"You guys'll do just great. Rod is talented and, Ally, you're so brilliant. You have nothing to worry about. My husband, Mr. Perfection, will have no trouble getting more contracts. There's already a bunch of stuff we're working on bids for."

"But this one was so big."

"Don't give it another thought."

I've always thought it strange that this glass-is-half-full person married someone like Rod, whose glass is usually half-empty. But I guess between them they end up with a full glass, so it works. Rod spread out sheets filled with numbers and figures on my dining-room table, while Jolene leaned against the wall and talked with me about baby furniture.

Some might say Jolene's nose is a bit too long and too pinched—aquiline, she calls it—and her lips too thin to be attractive by today's standards. Yet Jolene has an individuality. Her black plastic rectangular glasses only add to her look.

"But this was our chance at the big leagues," I said.

"You guys are already in the big leagues, especially you, Ally. What I want to know is how is the *Maddy?*"

"She's upstairs, barely speaking to me."

"No, I mean, your boat design, the *Maddy.*"

"Oh," I said, "I get to it every now and then." Named

for my daughter, the *Maddy* was the name I'd given to my design.

"Maybe this is what you and Rod should be working on. That's what I vote for and speaking of the other Maddy, would she mind if I went up and said hello?"

"She likes you. Maybe you can get her out of her mood."

After she left, Rod tapped the papers with his pen. "The problem is that we made the mistake of putting all our eggs in one basket."

He was about to say something more when the doorbell rang. My heart skipped a little beat. Mark had arrived. Self-consciously I checked my reflection in the hall mirror before I answered it. Hair a mess as usual. And why hadn't I at least put on a bit of makeup? And what was I thinking with this old sweatshirt? And why was I thinking about Mark in this way, anyway? As soon as Rod told him the news, he'd be gone and on to another job. A thought struck me as I opened the door: I should show him my *Maddy* boat design. I quashed that idea just as soon as I answered the door and he smiled down at me.

"Come in," I said. "Rod and Jolene are here already."

His eyes lingered on mine for a moment. "Must be a serious meeting," he said.

"Let me take your coat." He shrugged out of his green jacket. As I hung it up I noted the fraying around the collar. He probably needed this job as much as I did.

Mark hadn't even had a chance to sit down before Rod broke the news. "The project's been pulled out from under us. That's the reason for this meeting."

Mark stopped in his tracks. "Wow, how'd that happen?"

"Stupidity," Rod said. "On my part. I should have been more aware. It was my fault for hiring too fast and too soon, for hiring both of you before it was in the bag." Rod placed both hands flat on the table. Mark and I sat down next to each other and across from him. I was conscious of how close Mark was to me.

"Jolene and I have the money to keep both you and Mark for a couple of weeks if you want," Rod said. "There are a couple of other projects we're bidding on. I don't want to be unfair about this. You've done a lot of work already and I want to make sure you're fairly compensated."

Mark tapped his long fingers on the table. He took off his glasses, folded them shut and placed them on the table. I heard a thump from upstairs, wondered if I should run up there and check on Maddy, decided not to when I heard no more. Jolene was up there. Jolene could take care of it.

Mark said, "To say I'm not disappointed would be a lie. I've really enjoyed working with Ally on this." He seemed to move a little closer to me when he said this. I felt a heat rise in my face. He went on, "But, I've been in this business long enough to know how things work. And how sometimes they don't work the way we plan." Quietly, he added, "I know God will have something else for me…."

I was very still as I looked at a spot on the table. I flicked at it with a fingernail. His casual reference to God unnerved me. I'm impressed with people who refer to God in casual conversation, like a friend. Even when I did go to church regularly, God was never someone who looked out for the little things in life. Mark had stopped talking and was staring at the stack of computer printouts about Larry Fremont and Paul Ashton that I had placed beside my computer. Right on top was an article about Ashton's death with a full color picture of the man. I could kick myself for leaving these things right out there in the open.

Rod started in about future bids and direction while Mark stared at my printouts. His eyes were still on them when he said, "I could always go back to Florida. There might be work for me there...back at the marina."

I listened as Rod talked about future projects, about future ideas and directions. I could barely concentrate. More than anything I wanted to grab that stack of papers from beside my computer and shove it deep within the confines of my garbage can.

When we were finished I asked if anyone would like coffee. I'd made some.

"Not me," Jolene said emerging from the hallway and holding Maddy's hand. "But if you have any herbal tea, I'd kiss your little ears."

She signed as she spoke, and Maddy burst out laughing. Jolene's hair was held back, I noticed, by one of Maddy's pink butterfly barrettes. The three of us females went into the kitchen.

Jolene maneuvered herself into one of my kitchen chairs and we chatted about how she was feeling, signing at the same time so Maddy could be part of the conversation. When I first started studying American sign language, Jolene joined me. She's now fairly fluent and says she's planning to teach her own baby to sign before she even speaks.

Jolene was also with me when I first understood that Maddy was deaf. My baby didn't turn to loud noises. I would stand to one side of her and clap my hands and she wouldn't turn or flinch. I would stand behind her and call her name. Nothing.

I'd sit on my couch and rock back and forth and hope I had it wrong. Maybe it was something simple.

But I knew the worst one day while visiting Rod and Jolene and we were outside in the backyard. A truck rumbled by. Just as it neared the house it backfired. The sound was loud and excruciating. All of us jumped. Maddy sat in her high chair and grinned.

Jolene went with me the next day when I took her to the doctor and then the audiologist who confirmed my suspicion. She was profoundly deaf, cause unknown.

I knew absolutely nothing about deafness then or caring for a deaf child. I barely knew that there was a sign language. Through the years I've learned enough to fill a bookshelf. And I have. I have many books on deafness. I have pamphlets and printouts from the Internet, information on the deaf culture, signing, and hundreds of government leaflets and pamphlets on everything from implants to hearing aids to deaf literacy. Amassing this information, learning everything I can, meeting and talking with many deaf people has been, practically, my full-time job since Maddy was born.

My own career took a back seat.

By the time we went back to the dining room with mugs of coffee on a tray, Rod was hunched into his laptop, furiously clacking at the keys, and Mark had actually picked up the sheaf of papers I'd printed and was leafing through them. He raised his eyebrows at me when I came in.

I put the tray on the table and Mark asked me if he could see my boat design. I said, maybe. He carefully put the printouts back beside my computer aligning the edges and stacking them precisely. He patted the stack as a final gesture.

I stirred in milk and sugar and said, "Did you guys find anything?"

Rod said, "We've been surfing the Web for possible projects."

Jolene said, "I think you should work on the *Maddy.*"

"The what?" Mark said.

"Oh, it's nothing," I said.

"It's not nothing," Jolene said. "It's Ally's idea for a slick, one-person racing sailboat."

His eyes brightened. "Really? I'd like to see that."

"Maybe sometime. It's not ready. Have some coffee."

While we drank our coffee and Maddy played with her ponies on the floor, Mark tried to get me to talk about my design. Just like the previous day, when the meeting naturally came to an end, Mark didn't rise to leave first.

I handed Mark his coat, and said that I guessed the meeting hadn't been all that bad and how I was happy to get to work together for a little bit longer.

"I would like to continue working with you," he said.

"Well, yes, it's been fun."

He paused, took a breath and said quietly, "May I ask why you printed out all those news articles on Paul? If you don't want to answer, you don't have to. If I'm prying, that is."

"I was interested in the story."

"You always print off random articles?" He paused. "I'm sorry. I shouldn't pry."

"No, uh. It's okay." I paused. "Maybe you should know, especially because you knew Paul Ashton. Larry Fremont and I grew up in the same town."

His eyes widened.

"So, um, naturally, I was curious. His mother owned the mine that employed ninety percent of the people in our town."

"Did your father work in the mine?" His eyes were hooded when he looked at me and I couldn't read his expression. Did I imagine it or did his eyes take on an intensity that wasn't there before? Imperceptibly, I backed away slightly from him, but then I realized what it was. He knew Paul Ashton and Paul Ashton had died. No wonder he seemed intense, sad today. Anyone would, given those circumstances.

I shook my head, looked away from his piercing glance. "My father is a pharmacist. Fremont sent most of his business our way, so yes, I guess you could say that we, too, were employed by the Fremonts. My family moved to PEI when the mine closed." I tried to keep the nervousness out of my voice, but his eyes were frightening me. To change the subject I quickly asked, "How are the Ashtons today?"

He shrugged. "As good as can be expected, I guess. Paul's wife, Carolyn, is trying to be strong for the children, but it's hard on everyone."

"He had children?"

"Three. Two in their twenties, one single and one married, plus one in university."

"When's the funeral?" I asked. "Will it be at your church?"

"Yes, and it's not until next Saturday. There are some relatives coming from pretty far away."

I said, "They're saying now that he died from hitting his head on a coffee table."

He nodded toward my printouts. "So, I read."

"They're saying a heart attack or brain aneurysm could have caused him to fall initially."

"I know."

"I guess you would, because you know the family. I just find the whole thing a little odd, though. How many people die from falling and hitting their heads on the edges of coffee tables?"

He hesitated before he answered me. "You're not the only one who thinks it's odd."

"What do you mean?" I asked.

"Carolyn thinks it's strange, too." He went on. "The police say they're not ruling out 'foul play.'" He made quotation marks in the air with his fingers when he said the words *foul play.* "Carolyn says the police haven't been as forthcoming as she would like."

"Do you think it was foul play?"

He shook his head. "I don't know. Carolyn thinks perhaps the hotel is to blame. Maybe with the placement of their carpets. She's grasping at all sorts of straws."

Later after Mark left and Maddy had gone to bed, I couldn't sleep, like I knew I wouldn't. I draped my blanket over me like a shawl and went downstairs. Instead of working on the boat plans, because what was the point of that now—I opened a Web browser on my computer and began clicking through links. There had to be more than I was finding about the Fremonts. The Internet had lots of information. Trouble was, I wasn't quite sure where to look.

While Maddy slept soundly upstairs, I decided to do an in-depth Internet search, or as in-depth as I knew how to. But I had been over this territory many times. What I wanted was some mention of Tracy, of what happened on that bridge twenty-five years ago. But, there was nothing. Nothing at all. There never was. The Fremonts had covered up that one. They had effectively kept it out of the papers. If they could hide that one so easily, this one would be a piece of cake. They were used to this.

FOUR

We all called her "The Lady." She was tall and towered over all of us. But when I think back on it, I think it was her presence that was big, the way she would stand there, one hand on her wide hips, the other holding a cigarette, always unfiltered. I know this because she bought them from my dad's drugstore. Those were the days when drugstores still sold cigarettes.

The Lady owned the coal mine in my town, the one industry, the main employer. She was the lady of the manor and we were her feudal underlings. Eloise Fremont was the entire reason for the town and she knew it.

The town itself was one of those idyllic places along the Nova Scotia coast that tourists love to visit. They remark on the peacefulness of the place. They return home, remembering fiddle tunes and kilts and church steeples and green valleys and clothes on lines getting blown dry in the salt air. What is not so apparent to the tourists is the sludgy, undercurrent that runs beneath the whole of the town, a sewer that when it bubbles through to the surface leaves a taint on everything.

Eloise Fremont was that taint. The Lady.

When I was growing up, the expression was that "Coal is king," but the truth was, "Money is king."

Money was more important than standing up for the truth, than coming forward with the honest story. When my uncle, my father's brother, would visit from PEI, he said our town was the perfect example of the Golden Rule, the one who has the gold rules.

"It's not so bad," my father would say. "We have a good life here. You can't ask for a prettier place."

I remember The Lady coming into my father's store, her witch hair wild and unkempt and flaring out around her head like a lioness. She would stand there, a cigarette balanced on her lower lip or held between her first two fingers, her other hand braced against her square hips. She would squint as she surveyed the store, ready to criticize, ready to pounce. She always seemed on the verge of a loudly vocalized complaint. She would stand there and run her nicotine fingers through her hair or hold it up off her head with one hand while she punctuated her remarks with the other.

She wasn't an absentee landlord. Never that. Eloise was frequently in town, marching up and down the streets. She went to every town council meeting, every school-board meeting and made her opinions known. She complained heartily when she'd be asked to kindly extinguish her cigarette. Twenty-five years ago a person could smoke in most public buildings. Through the years I have wondered how she has fared with the stiffer nonsmoking bylaws. I always imagined her turning up her nose and pulling out her pack of cigarettes anyway.

The Fremonts were also a big part of our church. Her husband was on the church board, but curiously it was Eloise's viewpoints that got presented. Those were the days when church board involvement was only for the men. I think that infuriated her.

Our church building has been featured on many postcards. It has even ended up on a number of calendars. I might have one of these stashed away somewhere.

For the most part I ignored The Lady, or Tracy and I made fun of her. Her one son and only child Larry was in trouble a lot. She always bailed him out.

I don't remember much about Larry's father. He was a kind of nondescript figure who was overseas a lot on business. He died shortly after my family left.

Before everything came apart, my family went to that church every Sunday. Anytime the church doors were open, my family was there.

When I'd run home that day, stumbling, crying and sobbing out my story of what I'd seen on the bridge, my father called the police and the three of us went to the church. I can't really remember why we went there rather than to the police station, but my father had made a lot of phone calls while I sat in the kitchen, my head between my knees, choking and sobbing.

Someone must have told him to. That part's not clear in my memory. And when I've asked him about it in subsequent years, he's merely said, "I don't remember why. You're asking me to remember something long past, something better left unremembered in the first place."

Cars were in the lot that day, the doors were open and people were inside. I heard crying, wailing, really. The first face I saw on that day belonged to Eloise Fremont. She stared hard at me when we walked through the door. Our pastor was there, as were some of the church elders, along with the police.

At the end of the front pew, Tracy's mother was huddled, shivering, while the pastor's wife kept her arm around her. My mother went to her immediately.

Larry was there, too, silent and red-faced and sitting on the opposite side, his hands on his knees. Eloise said to my father in her loud voice, "You must have heard about the tragic accident. News travels."

My father said, "You know why I'm here, Eloise. I was told to come."

Everyone, including Tracy's mother, looked at him. No one talked to The Lady that way. Undaunted, my father continued, "My daughter saw what happened. She was in the graveyard. It wasn't an accident. Ask your son."

The place became dead quiet. Outside insects hummed.

"We did ask him," she said. "He tells a different story."

One of the officers opened a notebook. It had never occurred to me that people wouldn't believe me if I carefully told them what happened, what I had seen.

The moment I looked down when the bug bit my ankle became crucial then and during the hearing that followed. I hadn't really seen what I said I had seen because I hadn't been looking. The fact that Larry laughed merely became his word against mine.

But the police urged me to talk and I managed, with my father's help, to get out my story.

Later, I became the girl who was just trying to "make trouble" for the Fremonts. They had all sorts of reasons why I had made up such a story. I had a childish "crush" on Larry and when he spurned my affections, I made up a lie to hurt him. My father's business wasn't doing as well as could be expected, and we were taking it out on the Fremonts.

As the weeks passed, I simply stopped talking, which probably made it worse. My parents pressed, but I had clammed up and gone inside of myself. I was the "girl with the imagination," or "the girl who lied," and ultimately "the girl with all those emotional problems."

The Fremont spin was that it was nothing more than an accident. Larry and Tracy were on the bridge. They were arguing. Tracy leaned against the railing, which broke beneath her weight. Larry tried to save her as she fell. He felt terrible. Sick about it. The whole Fremont family did.

My entire teenage years were spent wondering if I really had seen what I thought I had. Whenever I lost something, misplaced something, forgot something or got something wrong, I would wonder—was I crazy, like they all said?

I sat at my computer now, looked out at the snow and wondered how it was that there was nothing about this anywhere on the Web. I glanced at the clock. No, it wasn't too late. I picked up the telephone. A few minutes later I was talking to my mother.

"Alicia!" she said. "How nice to hear your voice. We just this minute got in from church. How is everything there? How's Madison?"

"We're fine," I lied.

"Well, that's good. When are you and Madison planning to come for a visit? We'd love to see you."

"Maybe Easter break, if that works."

"Of course it would work. At the end of the month we're planning a trip to Quebec City. You remember how your father loves it there."

I said, "How are things at the store?"

"Just great, Alicia. Is there something on your mind?"

I've always wondered if my parents think my failed marriage had something to do with my "craziness." When my husband walked out on me and I was left with Maddy, my parents didn't seem, somehow, as *surprised* as I thought parents should be in a situation like that. My mother had merely sloughed it off, saying, "You've had such a hard go of things."

"Have you been watching the news?" I asked.

"What news, Alicia? You mean, about the weather? Yes, it is horrid, isn't it?"

"No. I'm talking about the Fremonts. Larry Fremont. Someone on his staff died under mysterious circumstances."

"It was a heart attack. Hardly mysterious." Her quick response proved to me that this little news item had not escaped her attention.

"It wasn't a heart attack, Mom. The man fell in his room and hit his head."

"Well, these things happen, don't they? People fall. They hit their heads. It happens."

"Not that often, Mom. How many people do you know that this has actually happened to?"

I could hear her sigh. "Alicia, this happens all the time. People fall in the tub and die. You read about that."

"Not healthy people, Mom."

There was a long pause. I could almost hear my mother thinking. "Alicia," she finally said. "Don't you think it's time to leave all of this alone? It was so long ago. It's a chapter your father and I have put aside. We've gone on with our lives. And you should, too. I'm sure the police are on top of this investigation."

"You mean, like they were the last time?"

I could hear her audibly sigh.

I said, "You're not the one everyone called crazy."

"You don't think we suffered, too? And your brothers?"

I couldn't let this go. "Maybe, just maybe it's time that certain people are brought to justice."

"You've held this resentment far too long, Alicia."

Resentment? It wasn't resentment that was fueling me. It was a desire to finally see justice done even after all these years. Because he'd killed someone again and was going to get away with it. Again. And I wanted people, all the people in my small town to finally not think of me as deranged. I wanted to finally be believed.

I must've paused for too long because she said brightly, "How did you manage with the snowstorm? Your father and I were going to call you. You really had the brunt of it down there. Not like us."

Nice change of subject, but that's what my mother always did.

"Mom." I was getting a headache. "Larry Fremont is not a good person. I think he killed that man. And I'm going to prove it." I have no idea why I said that. Did I want to shock her? Get her to believe me? And how on earth would I carry out such a task? I added, "Watching your best friend die is just something you just don't forget. Ever."

"Alicia, we love you. And we always will love you and Maddy, but sometimes our minds play tricks on us. What we're so sure we remember might not be the actual way it was."

I couldn't quite believe she was saying this.

She went on. "You were so sure about what you saw. Your father and I believed you at the time. Of course we did. You are our daughter, but, Alicia, the facts in the case just don't bear out your testimony. You know that by now, don't you?"

"No, Mom," I said evenly. "I don't know that. And I'm going to finally prove it."

FIVE

The following morning I dropped Maddy off at school and proceeded to Rod's office. I'd thought a lot about what my mother had said the previous night. She'd hinted at these things before, but she'd never come right out and said it. In times past she'd always said vague things like, "People don't always remember exactly the way they thought they did." It was always "People don't," rather than "You don't." Last night was as close as she'd ever come to saying, "What you thought you saw was not how it happened. So get over it."

When I got to the office of Maritime Nautical, Jolene was leaning against the counter and talking on the phone. I was surprised to see her and when she got off the phone, I told her so.

"Shouldn't you be home?" I asked.

"You mean, lying on the couch, eating chocolate bonbons and watching soaps with my mother?" She shook her shiny hair. "I'd go stir-crazy at home."

"I can't imagine your mother sitting and eating bonbons."

Jolene's mother, Beth, did not fit this stereotypical picture. She was a workaholic, who had had several careers in the time I'd known her, and was now working in real estate and doing well. Jolene was a lot like her: tireless, independent and energetic.

This morning Jolene wore a long-sleeved orange form-fitting T-shirt over a straight, black pencil skirt. She was the only woman I knew who could be so stylish in her last days of pregnancy. To her credit she'd at least ditched her black pumps and was barefoot in the office, her toenails painted a bright red and the dolphin tattoo on her foot clearly visible.

"But you're due any minute." I stared at her incredulously.

"Not any minute. Two weeks isn't any minute." She put her glass of apple juice down on the counter.

Maritime Nautical is in a storefront in a strip mall next to a marina. It's a small, square space with a tiny coatroom in the back and one washroom. Rod and Jolene had divvied up the space into several workstations. Rod had a large flat screen attached to his computer along the back wall next to a large drafting table. The walls were papered with boat designs and posters. Jolene's touch was evident in the plants which hung in the front windows. On her desk were a few African violets in full lavender bloom.

I took off my jacket and sat down at the computer I always used when I worked here, and thought back to my own last weeks while pregnant with Maddy. It was not as happy a time as this. Two weeks before Maddy was born, my husband had packed up the last of his stuff and moved out. He still has not met his daughter.

It was Jolene who helped me get through that hard time. Who told me I was smart enough to be a single mother. Who accompanied me into the delivery room and held my hand and coached me in the breathing. Jolene, who even then had wanted a baby of her own and had to watch her best friend become a single mother.

My mother came after Maddy was born. She had been solicitous and helpful, but ever since we had to leave Cape Breton, there had been this space between us. Last night I figured out what it was. She had never really believed me in the first place.

"Is Rod here?" I asked her.

"In the back. With Mark." She indicated with a nod of her head.

"Mark?" Mark was here? I ran a nervous hand through my hair. This reaction did not go unnoticed. She raised her eyebrows and then broke into a wide grin. "Ah-ha!" she said, pointing a perfectly manicured nail in my direction. "I thought so."

"What?" I hit the space bar and the computer came to life.

She followed me. "You're blushing."

"I am not," I retorted without looking up. "I do not blush. I am incapable of blushing. I have never been known to blush."

"Until now," she said with a wry smile. "I *thought* there was something between you guys."

"There is nothing between us guys."

"I see it on his face, too."

There was something on his face? "There's nothing to see. What do you mean you saw something on his face?"

She kept grinning.

I turned back to my computer and I went on, undaunted. "There are a thousand reasons why I can't be interested in Mark."

"Give me three."

"Well, for starters, we're different religions."

She gaped at me. "What do you mean you're different religions?"

"What I mean is that he has a religion and I don't."

"What's the big deal about that?"

I looked at her. "The big deal is that I can't go out with a guy who goes to church. Period."

She looked at me, a thoughtful expression on her face. "Ally Roarke, religion or no religion, maybe it's time you let somebody in. And maybe a bit of religion would do you good."

Rod and Mark emerged from the coffee room in the back and Mark stopped when he saw me.

"Hey, Ally. Hey, Jolene," he said, but his eyes were on me. "I wasn't sure you'd be coming in today." This morning he wore a loose-fitting off-white fisherman's sweater. It looked worn, but like all of his clothes, it looked good on him.

"I thought I'd come and download all the stuff I did for the project so we could send it back."

The truth was that I really didn't feel like staying home. I also had this other crazy, weird idea which involved Mark. I kept thinking about the promise I made to my mother, that I would finally see justice for Tracy's murder. Mark could help. Now I just needed to get up my nerve and get Mark alone.

My chance occurred around twenty minutes later when Mark pulled up a chair and sat beside me. He said, "I was at my parents' last night. Carolyn Ashton was there. She thinks that Fremont knows something about her husband's death, something he's not telling. She thinks someone may have killed her husband."

I stared at him with my mouth opened. I said, "And you're telling me this because…?"

He lowered his voice. "You said that you grew up with Larry. I was wondering if you could help us."

On the desk in front of me I tented my fingers, as if I was trying to appear thoughtful.

He said, "According to Carolyn, a whole lot of things don't add up. Apparently she wanted to go to Portland with her husband, but she got the definite impression from the Fremonts, Lawrence and his wife, that she wasn't welcome on the trip."

"That would be Belle," I said.

"Right. Fremont's wife. You know her, too?"

I said, "We grew up together. All of us, Larry and Belle and me. We all went to the same church. Belle's father worked in the mine, too." I played with my thumbs, nervously twiddling them. Belle was Larry's age, which is to say she was three years older than me, and like a lot of the girls at the time, including Tracy, Belle had her sights set on Larry. Belle, the pretty girl, the determined girl, was the one who finally nabbed him and all the family riches that came with him.

Mark said, "Carolyn had a strange visit from Eloise Fremont, of all people."

I raised my eyebrows. "Really?" Twenty-five years ago she'd paid our family a "strange visit" too. "What happened?" I ventured.

"Well, the gist of it was that she wanted to convey the family's sympathies to Carolyn. But Carolyn got the strong impression that she was being asked to keep quiet if she had any misgivings about the manner of her husband's death."

I hoped that my short intake of breath wasn't audible. Ask him, I told myself. Now, before you lose your nerve.

"You said the funeral will be at your church on Saturday?"

"Yeah. Why?"

"Would it be all right if...?" I paused, realizing what a crazy thing I was about to do. "If...um...could

I go with you to it, do you think that would be okay? Would you mind?"

He raised his eyebrows. "You want to come to the funeral with me?"

I nodded. Larry would most certainly be at the funeral and maybe it was time I confronted him. I would tell him I knew he was responsible for his coworker's death and see what kind of a reaction I got.

"Certainly." There was a kind of crooked grin on his face. "I'd be happy to escort you to that most auspicious occasion."

Later when I went to pick up Maddy and Miranda after school, I had to blink at my forwardness. Had I actually asked Mark out on a date? And was our first date to a funeral?

SIX

Saturday morning was gray and overcast. Quite likely it would snow again. I stood in front of my mirror, trying to get my hair right. I caught myself. I was primping? For a funeral? I had to shake my head a few times at that one. I'd scrounged a black pants suit from the back of my closet, and underneath I buttoned a plain, beige shirt to my neck.

I found a pair of earrings, tiny gold ones, not too much for a funeral. As I put them in, I thought about Larry and my fingers began to tremble. I dropped a tiny earring back and had to get down on my hands and knees to locate it.

Could I really stand up to Larry? I wouldn't know until I tried. Plus, Mark would be there with me. Did that thought make me more nervous or give me comfort? I didn't want to admit to myself that my feelings for him were growing. Mark had come in every day that week, but we didn't talk much about the Fremonts. The news was still calling it an accident. Paul Ashton didn't have a heart condition, but maybe he had had some sort of brain aneurysm which made him fall. Like my mother said, those things happened, didn't they?

I went to work every day and, needing to get my

mind off Larry and Mark, I spent some of the time working on my own design, the boat I'd been designing for the past ten years. I wanted it to be perfect. If I shaved off a bit, just a hair, from the leading edge of the keel, maybe it could go a hundredth of a second faster through the water. A hundredth of a second may not seem like a lot, but a hundredth of a second can be the difference between silver and gold on the dais.

"You know," Rod said, leaning over my shoulder on Friday, "maybe Jolene is right. Maybe this is a blessing in disguise. Maybe we need to work on this design of yours, get a few investors on board, get it into production."

I looked up at him. "It's not ready," I said.

"You need to trust yourself more. It's been more than ready for five years." I was never quite satisfied with it. Or maybe I was just afraid to let it go.

I couldn't tell him, I couldn't even tell Jolene—although I'm sure she suspected—that there is this part of me that's always afraid. I dream sometimes, and when I allow myself to, I dream that this design of mine will take off. Everyone who's anyone will be sailing them and there will even be class races with the *Maddy.* But what if I do this and it fails?

I gave myself one long last look and headed downstairs. As I pulled on my black boots, Mark's car drove up outside.

The house was quiet when I left. Maddy had spent the night at Miranda's. I locked the front door behind me. But no sooner had I settled myself in the passenger seat of his car than I put my hand to my mouth.

"Wait!" I said.

"What?" He was putting the car in gear.

"I think I forgot to lock my back door." Hurriedly

I unfastened my seat belt. "I'll only be a minute. Just let me check."

I raced up the sidewalk to my house, my heart pounding inside my chest, my lungs barely able to ingest air. My fingers shook as I attempted to unlock my front door. I put the key in wrong, fumbled with it for several seconds while shifting from foot to foot. And then I did it, I managed to get inside, and the moment I did, I shut the door behind me and leaned against it, shaking, shivering. I couldn't go through with this.

I couldn't go to the funeral. I couldn't come face-to-face with Larry Fremont. It was one thing to see his face in the newspaper and the news, but it would be quite another to look right into his eyes. And Eloise! I could still remember it like it was yesterday, her eyes as they bored into my own when I was thirteen and had just accused her son of murder.

"God," I prayed. "Help me. If You're there, if You're really there, will You help me just this one time?"

What I needed to do was to get out my cell from my purse and call Mark and tell him I couldn't go. Even though he was sitting in my driveway, I'd call him. I'd changed my mind. But as I was fumbling in my purse, there came a gentle knock on my door.

"Ally?" I heard him call. "Ally? Are you okay?"

I huddled there. I could almost hear him breathing. There was no way that he could know that I was right there on the opposite side of the door, huddling, shivering, almost in tears. And then, just as quickly, I straightened. What was I doing? The Fremonts couldn't hurt me. They couldn't.

And then I remembered what I had promised my mother, that I was going to prove that Larry killed that man. Isn't that why I wanted to go to the funeral in the first place? I was going to confront Larry now that we were grown-ups.

Gingerly, I opened the door.

"Ally?" He looked down at me, confusion on his face. He looked so kind but worried, as he stood there in his good suit, overcoat and hair neatly combed. I found myself wishing for him to take me in his arms and tell me that everything was going to be all right. I shrugged off that inappropriate feeling and said, "I'm okay. I checked the back door. It's locked. We're set to go."

I'm not sure he believed me, because his eyebrows knitted together as he regarded me. He walked close to me as we made our way down the walkway to his car. Our gloved hands brushed each other, but didn't quite touch.

The sun peeked out from behind a cloud when we pulled away from my street. Everything looked as if it were covered with a gloss of ice. By the time we were crossing the Mackay Bridge it shone blindingly down with all its bright yellow force.

We didn't talk much. Mark didn't even turn on the radio. When we got across the bridge, I broke the silence by saying, "Looks like it's turning into a beautiful day."

"It does." I looked over at the ships in the harbor, the sun twinkling off their sides.

Even though we were more than half an hour early for the funeral, we had to park nearly six blocks away. Our boots clacking on the pavement was the only sound as we made our way to the church.

"You'll get to meet my parents," Mark said. "I've told them all about you."

"You have?" My knees felt like jelly. "All good, I hope." And then I berated myself for that lame and overdone line.

"Of course all good. I've told them what a remarkable boat designer you are."

We were nearing the church and suddenly I felt panicky. Maybe it wasn't too late to back out. I glimpsed a coffee shop across the street with the Open sign flashing.

"Mark?" I slowed my steps. "I don't know about this. Seeing Larry again. You knew we grew up in the same town, um, and well, his family wasn't really well liked by the locals. By my family. There was a falling out. It would be weird to see him again. It's something I don't talk about very much. Why don't I wait for you over there?" I pointed. "I'll grab a coffee. And when it's over, you can drive me home. Or I can take a cab."

He stopped, looked at me doubtfully. "But I thought you wanted to go to this funeral."

I shook my head, swallowed. "I know. And I invited myself, and the whole thing's silly. I probably should never have suggested it."

"You don't have to be afraid, you know," he said.

I stood there, making no move to walk across the street. *Afraid?* How did he know I was afraid?

He said, "I'll be with you."

I looked at him. I needed to go to the funeral. If I didn't, I knew I would regret it. I steeled myself and we kept walking.

A block from the church, Mark said, "My father told Paul not to work for the Fremonts, that Lawrence Fremont was shady, but Paul said he considered it a challenge."

My brain was working overtime. "Really?"

"Larry Fremont doesn't have the best reputation."

"Right." I hesitated before I said, "But then, why would Larry, if he's that unscrupulous, hire a Christian like Paul Ashton? Why wouldn't he just hire one of his crooked buddies?"

"Carolyn has a theory about that. Fremont wanted to appear to be on the up and up, so he hires a Christian. It's sort of fashionable to get an evangelical Christian on your staff these days. Good for the image. But Paul told my father he figured it was God's will. He thought that God had taken him into the Fremont's employ 'for such a time as this.'"

"'Such a time as this'?"

"It's a story from the Old Testament. The book of Esther. Esther, a Jew, was part of the king's harem. When the Jews were being systematically put to death, Esther decided to go to the king and petition that the killing stop. When she was told that she could lose her life if she went to the king unbidden, she said quite possibly her whole reason for being in the harem at this time was 'for such a time as this.'"

I remembered. "Something like being in the right place at the right time."

"Right."

"I know that story. I used to go to church when I was little."

"But you don't anymore?"

"No."

"Because of what happened with the Fremonts?"

"Yes."

Mark offered his hand when we crossed a street. I took it and when we got to the other side he didn't let go. In fact, when we got to the church steps, he held it more tightly. "You're trembling," he said.

"This is a beautiful church," I said, ignoring his comment as we walked up the steps.

"It's a heritage church," he said. "All stone." Even inside, he didn't let go of my hand. I thought about the little white church on the river where I grew up. That church was white and light and full of air, this was stone and dark, yet lovely in its own way.

The place was full, but we managed to find a spot in a pew near the very back. Inside it was large and cavernous with lots of polished intricately carved cornices and woodwork. It smelled like dark carpets and heavy drapes. There was no casket up there. Just lots of flowers, a framed picture and oddly, a tennis racket. The body hadn't been released from the coroner's yet. Instead of waiting, they decided to honor him now. When they finally got the body, there would be a private interment. The paper had mentioned that.

I took off my wool gloves and laid them in my lap and looked at the program I'd been handed when we entered. As I sat there I realized just how long it was since I'd been inside any sort of church.

I expected organ music—serious, sonorous, solemn—instead music was being piped in, upbeat songs with a lot of strings and percussion. The program said that this was a mix of his favorite worship songs. While I waited I read through the program word for word. I learned that Paul Ashton had earned a law degree at the University of New Brunswick. He had worked at several corporate law firms in Nova Scotia and New Brunswick and was recently hired by Fremont Enterprises. He was survived by his wife, Carolyn, and three children—Melissa, Charles and Candice—and one brother, Raymond, and a sister, Cari, also his mother, Leila. I learned he loved tennis and played often.

I read that John Bishop would be giving a eulogy.

"Is that your father?" I whispered to Mark. He nodded.

The place was becoming packed and I was glad we'd arrived when we did. I read through the program again, then looked around me and studied what everyone was wearing. If I did this, if I concentrated on these things, I wouldn't have to remember that other funeral a long time ago, that funeral that had me weeping like a crazy person by the end of it.

I shut my eyes, but a tear leaked out of one corner. I quickly brushed it away with my forefinger while the loudspeaker singers sang about a home beyond the grave. Could God be calling me back? No. That song playing, the one that was making me cry, was for Paul Ashton and not for me. I brushed the feeling away, but it persisted.

Black-suited ushers were leading the Ashton family in. I watched his wife, Carolyn, walk down the aisle on the arm of a young man I presumed was her university-aged son. She was a tall, slender athletic-looking woman with short curly hair in a no-nonsense style. She wore a brown suit, but I got the impression that she would be more comfortable in tennis gear. I looked at the tennis racket at the front and felt a sadness.

The two daughters, Melissa and Candice followed. Melissa was the oldest and looked to be in her early twenties. On her arm was a young man, her husband, Peter, Mark whispered to me.

No one was openly crying. Yet in the funeral that is etched in my memory, everyone cried. Tracy's friends, all the kids from school, the teachers, her parents, no one stoically accepting the death of a thirteen-year-old as being "God's will."

While the family was seated at the front, I felt something settle like a rock in my stomach. I actually put my hand there. I had seen his face on posters. I had even seen him on the news. So I knew about his thinning hair, the paunch he'd developed. Too much rich food, I guessed. Larry Fremont was sitting in a pew on the far side of the auditorium. Next to him was his wife, Belle. Even though twenty-five years had passed, I would recognize her anywhere with her peaked nose and delicate heart-shaped face. Her chin-length hair was softly streaked with professional-looking highlights. Even from this distance her gold necklace glinted in the light of the chandeliers. She was staring straight ahead. I wondered if she, too, was thinking about that other funeral.

I felt my chest tighten. On the other side of Larry was his mother, Eloise. The woman had aged a lot and her large face hung in wrinkled folds. Her wild hair was completely white and elaborately styled on top of her head.

The last time I'd seen this woman was the day we were leaving our Nova Scotia home for Prince Edward Island. Boxes were everywhere and my father was stacking them in the back of our station wagon. My mother was holding a box with a lampshade balanced precariously on the top when Eloise pulled up in her sports car. My mother, ever the hospitable hostess, put down the box and walked over to where she had pulled up. The two of them stood there on the grass in the front-yard talking, Eloise holding her car keys and cigarette in her fist against her hip. She towered over my mother. I heard her say to my mother as I walked to the car:

"…You are making a good move, Abigail… If your girl can get the help she needs…"

I didn't stay around to hear the rest. I don't know what my mother said to her. By this time, I had climbed into the backseat of the station wagon and stayed there until Eloise drove away, sending up dust as she did so.

I closed my eyes briefly and listened to the soft funeral music. When I opened them, my gaze went to Larry again. I watched him lean into his wife, bend his head low to say something. Imperceptibly, she flinched and wiped her ear with the back of her hand, as if wiping away his whisper.

Someone got up now, a former colleague of Ashton's, and said, "He was uncompromisingly honest. And in a field such as law, this trait is admirable." I looked around for a chuckle, but there was none.

The next person went through all of Paul's accomplishments. I found myself thinking—Was that why he'd been…*murdered?* Because he was so honest? Maybe he'd found something askew in Larry's books, blew the whistle and had been killed because of it. These thoughts twirled through my thinking as I looked to the tennis racket at the front of the church. I blinked and forced myself back to the present. Carolyn dabbed at her eyes.

Mark's father was next. I thought how much he looked like Mark. He leaned into the podium with one hand and began haltingly at first, but then with more momentum about a family vacation taken by the Ashtons and the Bishops, and how Paul kept them all in stitches with his jokes.

John Bishop ended by saying, "I'm going to miss you, buddy. That tennis racket? Keep it handy. This game isn't over."

He left the platform and a man and a woman came up and had us all stand up and sing "Great Is Thy Faithfulness."

I felt my eyes welling with tears. I knew this song. I remembered it. There are times when I wish I had this kind of hope, the kind that these people had, that Mark has, the kind portrayed in the song that says that there is something beyond this life and it's a good something. It's the kind of hope that says everything will work out for the best, no matter what. I looked over at Mark, at the way he was singing.

Could this be mine? But what about what God had done to me? To my family? How could all of these people sing about a faithful God? I looked at the way Carolyn was singing. Her husband had just died, and yet here she was, singing about God's faithfulness.

Could I possibly have it all wrong? Maybe God wasn't responsible for every bad thing that happened.

I couldn't help it, my thoughts wandered back twenty-five years ago and I was wedged in the third pew from the front in a crowded and hot church with the casket of my former best friend at the front. My father had kept his arm around me the whole time. They had told me, warned me not to say anything. My mother hadn't wanted me to come at all.

"I'll stay home, I'll stay with you," she said.

"I have to go. I want to go. It's Tracy!"

"This whole thing has been too traumatic for you, Alicia. You've been through too much."

But I had gone. And had come face-to-face with an angry Eloise at the reception.

A few more songs, a few more eulogies and the memorial service for Paul Ashton was over.

We were standing and Carolyn and her family were being ushered out. She looked dry-eyed and strong. And there was something else there, too—determination?

Because we were near the back, it would be some time before we'd be able to leave. Much as I wanted to, it would not do to just get up and run. I stood and waited patiently, holding the program in both hands as hundreds of strangers filed past us.

And then there he was, passing not five feet from where I stood, I stared at him, but his eyes were straight ahead. Belle didn't see me, either, as she frowned and held on to Larry's arm. In an odd way, and one that I couldn't understand, Belle looked frightened and lost. Her fingers seemed to grip his arm too tightly. I watched as he patted her hand with his.

But Eloise saw me. Her aged, droopy eyes locked onto mine. She looked about to stumble. Her mouth opened in a little *o*. I looked down, thought I would throw up. When I looked back up, she was gone.

We were filing out now and Mark kept his hand on my back as we followed the press of people. As we made our way through the church, we kept pace with the crowd. We walked past the front door and down a wide hallway.

In no time, we entered a large, bright room and we were standing in a receiving line. I forced myself to remain calm. Mark was with me. This was a public place. Nothing could happen here, could it?

SEVEN

I stayed close to Mark as we waited in the line. Along the far side of the room, tables had been set out with plates of food and coffee and tea and punch. A number of people were already helping themselves and, even for such a solemn occasion, people drifted past us, plates piled high with food. The noise level in the place was beginning to rise.

Along another side of the room were several poster-boards with pictures of Paul tacked onto them and a few trophies on tables. Tennis, I imagined.

The line moved slowly, but soon I found myself just people away from Carolyn. And then I found her grasping my hand and saying, "You're Mark's friend.

"Yes," I said. "Mark and I work together. I'm so sorry for your loss."

"Thank you." She kept a hold of my hand with both of hers. Her eyes were red-rimmed but dry. This close I could see that her face was freckled and sun washed. She looked like she had just gotten back from some summery place. I guessed her age at mid- to late forties.

"I'd like to talk to you later," she said, still clasping my hand. "Maybe meet with you. I have some things I'd like to ask you, if that would be okay?"

"It would be fine," I said, wondering what Mark could have possibly told her about me.

She turned to Mark and said, "Wasn't your father great up there?" She paused and her eyes filled with tears. She blinked quickly and went on. "You and your parents have been so helpful to me."

"We're happy to help you. It's been such a shock to everyone."

She nodded. "They still don't know," she said rather desperately. "The police. No one is telling me anything..."

"I'm sure the police are working on it," Mark assured her.

"I hope..."

She said nothing more, and we moved on. Her children were next. The oldest one, Melissa was tall like her mother, but with lighter, longer, straighter hair. She, along with her husband, Peter, shook my hand and said they were glad to meet me. The couple looked as if they hadn't been married more than a couple of months. They stood so close together.

She gave Mark a brief hug. "Thanks for everything," she said.

We met the two younger children, Candice and Charles. Charles gave Mark a quick, perfunctory hug and pat on the shoulder, but Candice took hold of Mark, held on to him and wouldn't let go. He stroked her back while she wept on his shoulder. He whispered something to her that I couldn't hear. I stood aside and thought about the family vacations that the Ashtons and Bishops took. These two families were close.

It seemed to me that the hug went on a little longer than necessary. Later, when she let him go, she cast me a withering glance and I knew exactly what was going on. She was attracted to Mark and probably had been for a long time, and the look she gave me had with it a question. Who was I and why was I at this memorial service with her intended?

Well, I thought, who wouldn't be attracted to Mark? He was handsome, intelligent, gentle, caring.

We moved on to the refreshment table. Mark handed me a cup of tea in a tiny china cup. I didn't want it, but it gave me something to do with my hands. The whole idea of confronting Larry was a stupid one. What I really wanted to do was to get out of here. I smiled widely at Mark when he moved a little closer to me and suggested just that.

"How about we just leave? Grab a coffee some place else?"

I felt myself relax. That sounded absolutely wonderful and I told him so.

"I just want you to meet my parents first," he said.

"Okay."

His hand was on my shoulder and he led me to where his parents were standing near a table which held pictures and several tennis rackets.

John Bishop leaned toward me slightly and shook my hand, saying how nice it was to finally meet me. *Finally* meet me? I glanced up at Mark. Mark's mother was a tiny, plump woman who was very pretty. She took my hand and told me she was Leah Bishop and that it was a pleasure.

"We've heard so much about you," she said.

I nodded, gulped.

We were about to leave when I saw them. The entire Fremont contingent had been here the whole time. They were over in the corner behind the receiving line. Larry Fremont stared at me intently as he held a coffee on a saucer surrounded by several small sandwich triangles.

Next to him, clutching uncertainly to his arm and teetering on high heels, was Belle. He was saying something to her and she was nodding. Both of them were looking in my direction.

Even though her jewelry glinted and shimmered in the light, she looked uncomfortable wearing it. This was not the cocky Belle I remembered. This Belle looked almost cowed as she nervously wiped invisible strands of hair from her neck with her free hand. She was bobbing her head up and down at Larry's comments. When we were teenagers, Belle was always self-assured. She had determined early on that she would marry Larry. She didn't come from money. Her father worked hard in the mine to support Belle and her younger siblings. I don't remember what happened to her mother; I'm not sure whether she died or if they were divorced.

Behind Larry and Belle, Eloise was holding court, sitting on a chair, a cup of coffee in her large fingers. She was helping herself to sandwiches which were on a plate on a chair next to her. Even though she was much older, she was still larger than life. A cane leaned against the chair on the other side of her and like all the Fremonts, she glistened, from her silver hair to her jewelry. I did a quick calculation and realized that she would be in her eighties by now. Even from here I could see the enormous rings on her gnarled fingers. She'd seen me and was rising and moving her silk-enfolded bulk toward me, while using her cane for balance. She was as tall and imposing as she always was.

"Maybe we should go now," I whispered to Mark, but her voice boomed through our conversation.

"Well," she said. Her voice was strong, amazingly so for her age and all her cigarettes. Despite the cane, there was nothing frail about her.

If I looked hard enough at her now, her face changed and suddenly it was another reception a long time ago, and a much younger Eloise was coming toward me. She was wagging her finger at me and saying, "If you continue to make up the kind of stories that you are manufacturing about my son, Larry, it will come back to haunt you. You will pay the consequences." And then her eyes had blazed and she said quietly, sternly, "Get out of here!"

I had put my hands to my eyes and burst into tears. It was about this time that my parents came over and, because I could not stop crying, took me home.

Young Larry was there and as my parents took me out, he sneered at me as if to say, "See? I have people who stick up for me, people who stand behind me. And you don't."

Now twenty-five years later, I was at a different funeral and in a different place in my life, and Eloise was again barreling toward me. When she stood squarely in front of me, all black silk and jewels, I said evenly, "Hello, Eloise. It's been a while."

"If it isn't Alicia," she said. "Tell me, are you well?"

Mark took my hand, kept hold of it. But I kept my eyes on hers.

Was I well? A little jibe meaning, was I crazy? "I am well, thank you," I said. "You came all the way from Cape Breton to attend this memorial service?" I asked.

"I live here," she said. "That place is our summer home now."

When the coal mine closed, the Fremonts were not particularly popular in mining country. I could see why she would want to leave.

She opened her mouth to say something and then closed it, but it was time. I said, "I know what Larry has done. I know what he did twenty-five years ago and I know what Larry did this time." I was surprising myself with my boldness.

She regarded me for a few moments before she said, "You are most wrong," she said, her breath heaving. "You don't know how wrong you are about this. About everything. How wrong you've always been. You just can't see beyond your own hatred."

I smiled sweetly and held on to Mark's arm. Her sharp gaze shifted from my face to Mark's and she seemed to see him for the first time. She almost seemed taken aback by his presence. "And you, Mr. Bishop…" Her eyes flitted between the two of us and she added, "I see you two have teamed up."

I looked up at Mark, wondering at her turn of phrase. Was she suggesting that we were a couple? If so, that was a funny way of putting it. And how did she know Mark. I wondered briefly at this, but then I figured it out. She would know him because of the Ashtons. Of course.

Larry and Belle came over, Belle still clutching at his arm like a scared child. "Did I hear my name taken in vain?" he said. "Ah, Ally," he said extending his hand. He called me Ally. How did he know I'd shortened my name to Ally? I'd only been Ally since university. I shook his hand. His handshake was firm. "Here we meet at yet another funeral," he said. There were patches of gray in his hair and lines on his face. He looked every bit the successful businessman in his well-cut suit.

"We do, indeed."

"Mark Bishop," Larry said, extending his hand. "It's nice to see you again."

Mark nodded slightly and kept his lips close together when he said, "And you."

"You guys know each other?" I said. Why hadn't Mark mentioned this to me? I looked from one to the other.

"We've met," Mark said.

"At a function or two," Larry said, but was that a wink? "You look well," Larry said, turning his attention back to me.

Was this yet another jibe, like his mother?

"I am well. Thank you."

"That's good," he said. "That's very good."

"And you're doing well, Larry." I emphasized his name. "Taking care of the family business now, I see. Or should I say, your mother's business?"

He licked his lips, still patting Belle's hand. During this whole exchange Belle just stared at me, her eyes like arrows. Eloise was on the other side of Larry and was rapidly rubbing at the side of her bulbous nose.

"That boat business you're involved in seems to be doing okay," Larry said.

My grip on Mark's hand tightened. How could he possibly know that I was in the boat business?

"How do you know about me?" I stammered.

He winked. "Everyone knows about your little boat business."

Mark said, "Ally is an expert in her field. One of the finest engineers I've worked with."

Eloise said, "So that's how you two teamed up. You're working together."

I stared at her. What she was saying was not making sense. Maybe her mind was going. That would be a blessing, I thought.

At about this time Belle spoke for the first time, "Hi, Ally." Her voice was hoarse and there was a strange luminosity in her eyes. Was she drunk? Is that why she hung uncertainly on to her husband's arm? Is that why he patted her hand like a father would a child's?

"Hello, Belle."

Belle said, "And your little daughter, Madison? How is she?"

I felt like I had been punched. I knew what this was. The entire Fremont clan was reminding me that even after all these years they had the upper hand. They knew all about me. They knew I'd shortened my name to Ally. They knew I designed boats. They knew I had a daughter named Madison.

"How do you know about my daughter?" I choked, covered my mouth. I barely got the words out. Mark let go of my hand and put his arm around me. I was grateful for his presence, his closeness. Belle didn't answer. She whined to Larry, "I need a drink."

In a condescending voice he said, "There'll be no drinks here, dear."

Nevertheless, she let go of his hand and tottered to the refreshment table. Eloise followed. Before Larry turned away, he said to Mark, "I'd like for the two of us to get together. To talk. Can we arrange that?"

Mark looked down and shook his head. Larry clapped him on the shoulder and said, "Well, you think about it. I better be getting back to my ladies." He drifted off and I stared after him open-mouthed and then up at Mark, who shook his head as if to say, "I don't know what that was about, either."

At the refreshment table, Eloise was talking very rapidly to Belle. From the way Belle recoiled and swung her arm away from Eloise when the older woman tried to touch her shoulder, it was obvious that there was no love lost between them.

Mark's hand was on my back and he whispered

down to me, "How 'bout we blow this popsicle stand and get that coffee now?"

"That is the best offer I've had all day," I said.

"Get away from these crazy people," he added.

We said a last goodbye to his parents and to the Ashtons, then made our way through the doors and to the outside, his hand comfortably on my shoulder the whole time.

Outside, the sun had disappeared and the smell of snow was in the air. Wind blew against our faces like frozen rags. It was coming right off the water and the sound of it made talking difficult. I wanted to ask him about Larry, but there was something in his eyes that made me hesitate. I didn't know why. Instead, I said, "It was so sunny when we got here."

He muttered something that sounded like, "Right," but I couldn't be sure. He didn't take my hand this time, and there seemed to be some deep pain on his face.

"Are you okay?" I said.

He was shaking his head. "It just doesn't make sense. None of it does."

"Funerals are so hard, I know," I said. "Especially when it's the death of someone young and healthy."

"I'm not talking about that."

"What are you talking about, then?" We were at a street corner and stopped while we waited for the light to change.

He looked at me and frowned. "You're not the only one who has had unfortunate dealings with Larry Fremont." He spat out the sentence.

"I gathered that from the conversation. Sounds like he wants to talk to you. What was that all about?"

The walk light came on. We stepped out onto the street. He said, "We were in a business together."

"You were?" Even though we were in the middle of

the road, I stopped, stared at him with wide eyes "You were in business with Larry? When was this? You didn't tell me."

He took my hand and led me across. "We were in business together. And then he pulled out his money..."

He didn't say anything more. So, I finished his sentence for him. "And you were left hanging."

"That's why my father warned Paul not to work for him."

"So that's why Eloise knew you, and Larry said he wanted to talk to you. Are you going to meet with him? Maybe he's going to give you back your money. Ha, ha." Maybe that's why he didn't tell me any of this when I told him I grew up near Larry. There was an element of embarrassment or shame.

He shook his head and said wryly, "I won't meet with him. I have no desire to, not after what he did. But..." He paused. "I really struggle with this whole thing. I'm trying to do the Christian thing, but right now I just feel like I don't want to have anything more to do with that man."

"Wow!" I still couldn't get my head around this whole thing. "So we both have had a problem with Larry."

"It would appear so."

"We have a lot in common."

"More than you know," he said.

We were walking along the harbor now and tiny, white bulbs in the gusty skeleton trees along the water gave the place an enchanting feel. To our left were the lights from the boats in the harbor. Our boots click-clacked on the well-shoveled sidewalk and our breath came out like cold smoke. He said to me, "So, that's my Larry Fremont story, money ventured and then withdrawn, with bank loans still outstanding. What's yours?"

I shook my head. "It would take too long."

"We've got all afternoon."

We were between buildings now, which cut the wind and made talking easier. He said suddenly, "Carolyn thinks someone killed her husband. She can't get a straight answer from the police. She thinks her husband found out something about Larry's finances, something he wasn't supposed to know…."

I nodded.

"But the police aren't saying one way or the other."

I added, "I guess they have to be careful until they get all their ducks in a row."

On the corner was what looked like a café. "This place look okay to you? You need to warm up. You're freezing."

"I'm okay."

The café we entered was dimly lit, rather shabby looking with a worn barn board floor and rustic wooden booths. An old-fashioned jukebox leaned against one wall. The place looked like it had been lifted out of an old movie. Its walls were covered with posters. I glimpsed James Dean, Marilyn Monroe, several of Elvis. The place had a somewhat dingy feel to it, but I was ready to warm up and eat whatever was put in front of me. We chose a booth in the back and slid in across from each other and pulled off our gloves and toques and piled them beside us.

A waitress with a glimpse of a butterfly tattoo underneath the sleeve of her T-shirt came over with a coffeepot. She poured two coffees and plopped down menus in front of us and left with barely a word. We looked around us and commented on the place, but didn't resume our conversation until after we had placed our orders.

"Does Carolyn have any proof of anything?" I whispered across at him.

He stirred a spoonful of sugar into his cup and shook his head. "She's looking through his computer now."

"Does she think Larry killed her husband?" I asked tentatively.

He looked up. "She wouldn't admit that, but I have an idea that's exactly what she thinks."

"How about you?"

He looked down into his coffee and said evenly, "There is no doubt in my mind that he's dishonest and ruthless, but I can't see him committing murder."

We chatted a bit more about the case, speculating on what Paul may have found that got him killed. The waitress brought our food, and we stopped talking until she left us alone again. There were two other groups of patrons in the restaurant. Neither was close enough to hear us.

"What about your story?" he asked. "What's your Larry Fremont story?"

I cut my chicken wrap into halves, put down my knife and stared into his eyes. I said, "I agree with Carolyn. Larry *is* capable of murder. I know it."

He held his hamburger still.

I took a breath and said, "You want to know my story? Well, here it is: Twenty-five years ago I saw him kill my best friend."

He leaned toward me, eyes wide behind his glasses.

"I was thirteen years old," I said. "And no one, not even my parents, believed what I saw. And so Larry went free. And he continues to walk free. I know that he is quite capable of killing anyone who gets in his way."

While we ate our lunch, I told him the whole story, how I'd stood behind the gravestone and watched Larry push my best friend off the bridge. How he had laughed.

"In the time it took me to run home, the Fremonts had been able to spin the whole thing in their favor."

I was suddenly not hungry. I looked at the remnants of my food and said, "Sometimes I even wonder myself.

Did I really see it? But then I remember that laugh. If it was an accident, like they all said and something that he felt so terrible about, he wouldn't have laughed. Sometimes I dream about it. I think I shall hear that laugh until the day I die."

"I'm so sorry, Ally. What a thing to go through." His eyes were gentle when he looked at me.

I took a sip of my coffee. Another couple had arrived and sat at the table directly behind us. They seemed engrossed in each other. Nevertheless I kept my voice down.

I continued, "At that funeral I was so upset and I couldn't stop crying and talking about Larry. That's when the rumor started—I'm sure by the Fremonts—that I was unbalanced, that I 'was a mouthy kid and had problems.'"

"You? Mouthy?"

That got a smile out of me. "I was never a mouthy kid. I've always been on the quiet side. Still am, sort of. My parents went to the police in Sydney, the nearest big city from where we lived, but they seemed powerless. It was me against the Fremonts. Who would you believe? A thirteen-year-old girl or the rich family who runs the church and provides jobs for everyone?

"It didn't happen right away, but over the next few months we began to be shunned. My dad was suddenly asked to step down as church elder and they found 'someone else' to take my mom's Sunday-School class. The church didn't stick up for my family. My dad's business began failing. That's how powerful the Fremonts were. My dad got a job on Prince Edward Island. When we moved, I never went back to church. My parents didn't, either, for a long time. But then they started again. They've regained their faith, or maybe they never lost it. That didn't happen to me. No one believed me."

"I do."

He said it simply, matter-of-factly and his voice was so tender that I wanted to cry. He reached across and unexpectedly touched my cheek. It was a caring gesture, and I didn't want to read any more into it than just a friend comforting a friend.

"Thank you," I said, "but you don't know me very well."

"I know you well enough," he said. "You're talented, smart, a wonderful mother and honest. You are a very honest person."

I felt embarrassed, shy. He moved his hand away from my face.

"What happened to Tracy's family?" he asked me.

"I don't know. They stayed, I think."

"This whole thing has turned you into a sad person," he said.

"I suppose." I picked up my sandwich, then put it back down. I just couldn't eat. "Going to the funeral today just opened up a lot of old wounds," I said.

"But for a wound to heal it needs to be opened up, cleaned out and disinfected."

"Sounds painful," I said without enthusiasm.

There was a tinkle of laughter from another booth.

He nodded. "Sometimes it is. But God can be counted on to be there."

"I'm not so sure about that. He wasn't there for me."

But even as I said it, the words felt like dry bread in my mouth. I'd been spouting this line for so long that I'd come to believe it. But was God trying to break through to the hard place in my life, even as I sat here in this restaurant with Mark?

That was the one fact I didn't tell Mark, one little piece of the story that I left out—Larry had threatened me. When I'd burst into uncontrollable weeping at Tracy's funeral, it wasn't solely that I was missing Tracy. My tears had been brought on by something entirely different.

What made me cry had happened the night before.

I had been alone and was walking toward the footbridge. The round ball of evening sun hung low in the sky behind me, and I carried a bunch of flowers that I planned to leave on the footbridge in honor of Tracy.

I had plucked the daisies from my mother's garden without her seeing. I'd also cut off a long length of purple grosgrain from her sewing basket. My bouquet needed more, however, so I'd gathered handfuls of sweet peas from my mother's oblong garden down at the front of our driveway. Tied all together they wouldn't look too bad, I hoped. I laid out my offerings on my bed.

And then I shrieked.

A grimy, brown garden slug slipped off one of the daisy stems and onto my hand. My yowl was followed by a kind of a guttural "ohh," as I batted my hand wildly and the slug fell onto my bedroom floor. My mother was at my door, but I had locked it.

"Alicia? Are you okay? What's wrong?"

I forced myself to be calm while the slug made its slow and icky way across the carpet.

"I'm okay," I called to her.

She left and I managed to gather up the slug in about ten tissues and flushed the wad down the toilet. If it plugged up, my dad would deal with it.

After supper—which was a somber affair, this being the night before Tracy's funeral, I climbed out of my bedroom window with my flowers.

Because it was June, it was still light out.

I set off for the footbridge, carrying my garland in

both hands like a bride. At the place where the path narrowed, I heard a rustling in the underbrush. An animal, I thought. Maybe the neighbor's dog had followed me. I stopped, looked over.

No, it wasn't a dog. It was a person in all that blue, flowering underbrush. My first thought was Tracy! It had to be Tracy! Maybe she hadn't died in the water! Maybe she'd floated downstream and had crawled through the trees and the bushes and now she was here, limping through the vetch. She was cold and confused and had been living out in the woods all this time.

But when the figure emerged, it wasn't Tracy who stood there in the fading sun of the June night. It was Larry.

Larry!

He and I were the only two people in the world who knew what really happened. I screamed and turned to run. But he was faster and came and grabbed my shoulder. I dropped my flowers onto the ground and they scattered out of their ribbon. I tried to shrug out of his grasp.

"Wait, Alicia," he said. "I have to talk to you." He let go of me and in that instant I took off. He grabbed me again, this time fiercely and with both hands. He was older, bigger and stronger. I was no match for him. "Stop," I pleaded. "Let me go."

"I can't," was his simple and straightforward reply.

Directly behind me was the footbridge. I knew he could pick me up, take me there and throw me off, the way he had Tracy. I began to be more afraid than I had ever been in my life. "What do you want?" I managed to blurt out.

He didn't say anything, just held my shoulders and stared down into my face, his mouth working as if he wanted to say something, but couldn't manage to find the right words.

It was a hot and muggy night and a mosquito bit my knee. I didn't bend down to swat at it.

"What do you want?" I asked again.

He came so close to me and said, "I want you to stop lying about me, Alicia." His brown hair was long then and hung greasily in his eyes.

I was hot and cold at the same time, but when I opened my mouth to say something, nothing came out. I shook my head.

"Why?" His face was red, blotchy. He looked in pain. "Why are you doing this? That's all I want to know. Why are you doing this? What did I ever do to you?"

His grip on me loosened and I bent to retrieve my scattered flowers, swatting at the mosquitoes that were gathering. I rose, met his eyes and said, "Just leave me alone."

"No!" He said. "You leave *me* alone. I didn't do it. You *know* I didn't do it."

I finally found my voice. "Yes, you did. I saw you. I was in the graveyard. I saw everything. Don't deny it." I glanced across the footbridge to where the fading sun cast long shadows across the graves.

Larry's eyes looked wet, as if he'd been crying. Years later I would wonder if he had been.

I held what was left of Tracy's bouquet to my chest.

"Please…" he pleaded.

"I saw you kill her!"

He got angry then. His eyes bulged and his nose dribbled. He swiped at it with his thumb. In that moment he looked like a monster to me. I turned to run and he grabbed me by my shoulder. I nearly fell, but managed to stay standing.

His horrible red face was inches from mine when he said, "Leave me alone…or—or else…"

"Or else, what? You'll kill me, too?"

"Right!" His grip on me lessened for just a moment. "Just like I killed Tracy!" His voice was vicious and fierce and mean, but his grip on me lightened. "Exactly the same way," he added.

I took that opportunity to break away from him.

"I'll find you," he called after me as I ran. "No matter where you go or where you are. I'll always know where you are. If you say one word…"

All through the decades that followed, I believed him.

After Tracy's funeral Larry was shunted off to Europe to be with his father. In the fall he was back at his private school in Sydney, Nova Scotia, and by the following year, we were living on Prince Edward Island and attempting to start over.

Watching your best friend die does something to you, something that can't be taped up or easily repaired. I disagreed with Mark. This is something that can't be fixed. It's a sore that keeps festering, no matter what you do. Even God had not been able to mend this. Would God be able to help now?

I thought about these things as I changed out of my funeral suit and into a comfy sweatshirt and a pair of plaid pajama pants. I made my way down to my kitchen.

The house was strangely quiet without Maddy. She was with Miranda, and was probably having a fun night. She would be going to church with Miranda tomorrow.

Maddy had begged, pleaded, and I had given in. I couldn't explain it. For so long I'd had my back turned to God, but now, since the funeral, since meeting Mark and thinking about all that had happened again, I hadn't exactly turned to face God—to accept Him—but maybe I had turned halfway there. If I looked hard, I could see Him out of the corner of one eye.

"You may go to church," I had said.

"Goody!" She had sighed, then, clapping her hands, she'd run upstairs to get ready.

So I was alone. Again. I sighed and placed my restaurant carton with half of the chicken wrap I hadn't eaten earlier into the fridge.

I would be lying if I said my feelings for Mark weren't growing. There was this weird sort of giddiness about me whenever I thought about him. Should I allow these feelings to continue? Was there a chance for us? Or do I nip them in the bud? Mark knew my whole story now and why it was I'd turned my back on church, and yet it didn't seem to matter to him. And we *did* have Larry Fremont in common. A bit of a smile crossed my face when I thought about that. I closed the fridge door and sat down at my kitchen table and glanced through the newspaper. Nothing about Paul Ashton or Larry Fremont. I folded the paper and put it aside.

I picked up the phone to call Jolene. My good friend would have advice for me, I was sure. I needed to kick back and tell her everything. When I picked up the receiver, I heard the beeps signifying that I had a voicemail message. I pressed the button.

"Alicia? This is Eloise Fremont. I know you're not going to believe me when I say this, but it was good to see you today…"

I sat frozen to my chair.

"It's imperative that I speak with you immediately. I can't stress this enough. Can you call me at your earliest convenience?" She recited the number.

I didn't write it down. I wouldn't call her. She was the last person I wanted to talk to. I deleted the message.

I called Jolene and told her about the funeral, meeting Larry after all this time, the confrontation with

Eloise. I also told her that Eloise had called me. "You remember my telling you about Eloise?"

"She actually called you? What did she want?"

"I don't know. Probably to tell me to leave Larry alone again. I stood up to him at the funeral. I'm sure that's what this is all about. Did you know that Mark and Larry Fremont were once in business together?"

"What? Are you serious?"

"I am. The Fremonts are sort of venture capitalists, among other things, and well, I guess Mark persuaded the Fremonts to invest some of their capital into his boat-designing business. But Larry pulled out and left Mark holding the financial bag. I didn't get all the ins and outs of it. Mark seemed reticent to talk about it and I guess I can't blame him."

There was silence on the other end. Finally she said, "Are you sure about this?"

"Quite."

"Well, um. That's odd. When was this?"

"He didn't say."

"I only ask this because I don't think there was anything about it in his résumé."

"This would be stuff you don't normally put in a résumé," I said, "especially when you're trying to put your best foot forward. You usually don't mention past failures in a résumé."

"There's something else, and this is really weird, Ally, but why would he need Fremont money when he has Longstreet money coming out of his ears?"

My eyebrows scrunched together. "What is Longstreet money?"

"You don't know?"

"Know what?"

"His mother is a Longstreet. That's her maiden name

and they are like the Fremonts, a name to be reckoned with in Nova Scotia."

"Jolene, I have no idea what you're talking about."

"Why don't you come over?"

Half an hour later Jolene and her mother, Beth, were giving me a tour of Jolene's new nursery. Beth, as much as Jolene wouldn't admit it, is just an older version of Jolene. Tall, smartly dressed, she carried herself with the same kind of pride that Jolene did. Beth had taken a few weeks off work to be with her daughter and new granddaughter.

It wasn't until after we'd consumed taco salad and Beth had ensconced herself in her room to catch up on her work that I asked Rod about Mark. He found a file and placed it down on the kitchen table. "I don't know if I should be showing this to you or not..."

"Oh, let her see it, Rod," Jolene said, rising and getting out her herbal tea collection. "People post their résumés on the Web now, for goodness' sake."

He patted the file folder and got up. "Okay, then, I'm just leaving the file here. I'm getting up and going to the other room. I have no idea what you're going to do with it."

"Rod, don't be so dramatic."

When Rod walked out of the room, Jolene and I grabbed for it at the same time. We sat close together at her kitchen table, our heads together. It was a professionally done up résumé of four pages. The last place Mark had worked was in a marina in Florida. But we knew that. Before that he was employed as a boat builder in North Carolina. Jolene was right. There was no mention of any design business gone bad that either of us could find.

I also saw that he had just returned to Nova Scotia

four months ago. I began to wonder when his business venture with Larry had happened.

"Do you ever wonder about him?" Jolene said. "Like how come he's not married? Maybe this little document will tell us why."

"People don't put marital status on résumés anymore," I countered. "It violates the privacy act or something."

She picked up the first of the four pages and brought it close to her face. "Still, you'd think…"

I read through his education page. He wasn't an engineer like Rod and me, but he had a BA in Business and a Diploma in Design.

"He could've been an interior decorator," Jolene said. "What a catch. Every woman wants an interior decorator for a husband."

I put the sheet of paper on the table and stared at her, stone-faced. "Jolene. Don't get ahead of yourself. We haven't even had a date yet."

"Oh." She said innocently. "I wasn't talking about *you,* I was saying in general. Every woman would love to be married to a decorator. And I also beg to differ. Yes, you did have a date."

"Not a real one."

"And what was today all about?"

"A funeral is not a date."

I picked up the résumé again and found myself reading through his career goals and objectives.

It looked as if Mark took the design course to specifically work on boat interiors, but again nothing about a business. In fact, one of his career objectives was to set up his own boat interior design business.

"What about the Longstreets?" I said, putting the résumé back down. "How do you know he's related to them—whoever they are?"

"When I heard that his mother's maiden name was Longstreet, I put two and two together."

"And came up with five. I've never heard of them."

Dimly from the other room, I could hear Beth on the phone, wheeling and dealing house prices the way she did. Rod still hadn't returned. I said, "Just knowing someone's name is Longstreet doesn't necessarily mean they're related to some family named Longstreet."

I turned to the last page and read, "References supplied on request." I asked, "Did Rod request these?"

She rested her head in her hands. "You know, I don't think he ever did. Mark just seemed so good, too good to be true, actually. And he worked out well. Until we lost the contract."

Thoughtfully, I put the résumé down on the table.

Too good to be true.

Two phone messages were waiting for me at home. The first was from Mark. I was very still while I listened. He sounded out of breath. "I've been thinking a lot about what we talked about today, in particular about Larry Fremont. I have a cousin who's a police officer in Sydney. The two of us spent about an hour on the phone. If it's not too late when you get in, can you call me? This is important and could open up everything. We need to do something about Larry Fremont before it's too late."

My thoughts about Mark twisted and jumbled around in my brain. Why had he spent an hour talking with his police officer cousin about Tracy's death? And why hadn't he put his business venture with Larry Fremont on his résumé? The simple explanation was that he just didn't want to. Embarrassment? Maybe. And even if his mother was a Longstreet, it couldn't be *the*

Longstreet family that Jolene had told me about. And if it was, did that even mean anything?

I looked at the clock on my wall and hesitated. Was eleven-ten too late to call him? Probably. Reluctantly, I decided to wait until tomorrow.

The second message was from Eloise.

"This is the second time I've called you. I don't know where you could possibly be. I can't stress how *important* it is for you to get in touch with me immediately." She left her number—again, which I ended up erasing—again, but not before I'd given it a bit more thought than I had the first time she called. I actually did think about calling her. For half a second.

I wrapped a blanket around my shoulders. I was conscious of how cold my house was as I made my way down the stairs and into my basement. Somewhere down here was my old diary.

When Tracy and I were friends, we wrote in each other's diaries, and then when Tracy was no longer my friend, I wrote long and hard about that. I remembered writing pages and pages about the accident on the footbridge.

Where was that diary? It was freezing and despite my fleece track suit and the blanket, my teeth actually chattered. To save money I never kept the heat on down here. I sifted through box after box, looking for that elusive diary. When was the last time I'd even seen it? Way before Maddy was born, at least.

I was shivering, damp and cold by the time I finally located it. It was at the very bottom of a plastic hinged box filled with old photographs and school albums. It was a box whose contents I'd thought about tossing on more than one occasion.

The diary was pink and had a little strap which

went from back to front and locked. It was locked, of course, and I had no idea as to the whereabouts of the key. I put the rest of the stuff back in the box, shoved it back into place. Holding the diary close to my chest, I ventured up the cold stairs and on up to the warmth of my bedroom. I easily cut the strap with a pair of scissors and, safe and warm under my covers, I opened to the first page. Out fell a tissue-wrapped lump. I knew what this was. Two summers before Tracy died we had gone shopping for lockets. My mother was with us and helped us pick them out. Then we'd had our pictures taken in a mall kiosk and cut them to fit inside.

I opened it up and looked down at the picture. There were the two of us, smiling, our faces together. I closed it and wrapped it back up. I opened the diary at the first page.

Tracy's writing gave me a pang. Her penmanship was circular and loopy and she always dotted her *i*'s with little hearts.

Most of those early entries were about all the boys we both thought were cute.

Did you see that new guy? Isn't he a doll? Alicia doesn't think so. Ha, ha.

And then my writing: *Tracy thinks EVERY boy is cute, I think she's boy-crazy.*

I'm not boy-crazy, you are.

It went on like that, day after day: *In two weeks we go to church camp! Yay! I wonder if there will be any cute boys there.*

I blinked at my own boy-craziness. Had we really been that bad? Apparently.

I wrote in great detail about a school dance I wasn't allowed to go to and how unfair that was. Tracy wrote about her language arts teacher and how she hated doing her homework for that class. I wrote directly underneath about how much I disagreed. *I like writing stories,* I wrote.

I considered that as I bent over the diary and pulled the blanket around my shoulders. I used to write stories, yet I had gone into a math field—engineering.

More entries: the things we did, the places we went, the boys we liked. Increasingly, toward the end of the journal Tracy's entries were more and more about Larry.

And then abruptly, Tracy's entries stopped. Then there was a time lapse, a whole lot of blank pages, or pages written only by me. A lot of my entries were about my longing for Tracy, my missing our friendship.

I don't know why she's not being my friend anymore.

It's not fair.

She's acting so weird.

In school I asked her why she wasn't my friend anymore. She said she was in love with Larry. I told her that I thought Larry was dangerous.

Dangerous? Had I written that?

The school year before she died we barely spoke to each other, yet I was still desperate for her.

I don't understand why she's ignoring me, I wrote. *I asked Wanda if she knew. Wanda's main friends with Tracy now and Wanda said, well, if you don't know...* I ran my fingers across the page and tried to place Wanda. As much as I could remember, she was one of those rare girls who moved freely between the popular and unpopular girls.

I was getting near the end of the book. I turned the page and read what I had written: *Wanda told me that Larry is the main reason Tracy is not speaking to me. She said that Tracy was mad because I thought Larry should go with Belle and not Tracy.*

Later I read:

Tracy is not allowed to go out with Larry, because Larry is so much older. That's what Wanda told me. Wanda said that Tracy is not speaking to me because she thinks I told her father that she was going out with Larry secretly. But I didn't. Why would I go up to someone's father and tell them that? I didn't. I need to tell Tracy this.

The last six pages were devoted to my account of what had happened on the bridge. I read it through in its entirety a couple of times. Yes, in all these years, I had remembered everything correctly.

The bedside telephone woke me.

"Hello?" The little locket fell onto the floor beside me. It clattered to the floor and I clamored for it at the same time as I reached for the phone. Light was filtering through my curtains. It was morning. Maddy? She was at Miranda's. Was she okay?

"Ally?" It was Mark.

I sat up suddenly, cleared my throat. "Hi," I stammered.

"I hope I didn't wake you."

I coughed, choked on my cough, said, "Not at all."

"I was wondering if you and Maddy would like to come to church with me this morning."

"Maddy's at a friend's house."

"How about you? Would you go with me?"

I put my hand to my forehead. "Um. No. I should be here when Maddy gets home."

"How about going with me to Sydney for a couple of days then?"

"What?" I put a hand to my face. I felt flushed. Had I heard him right?

"...I was thinking about what you told me yesterday. All of what you told me yesterday. I called you last night. Did you get the message?" He sounded out of breath. "I think the police should reopen the case of your friend Tracy. I told you about my cousin who's on the police force in Sydney? I have an idea I want to run by you."

"Um." I couldn't think straight. I held the locket in my hand, noticing how cheap it was, how tarnished and how flimsy. When we had purchased them, we thought we were buying expensive gold. I placed it on my bedside table.

He went on, "This is serious, Ally. I don't think we should let this go. And now he's doing it again. Carolyn wants to hire a P.I. I told her, let me look into it a bit for you, I've been on the phone with her and with my cousin going over those old police reports from the time your friend died."

I gripped the phone.

"...that's why I'm wondering if you'd like to go to Sydney with me for a couple of days. If we ever want to have a hope of bringing Larry down, this might be it." He seemed breathless, and as he talked I was becoming more and more confused.

My thoughts were swimming. I picked up my diary from the floor. "But it was more than twenty-five years ago," I stammered.

"There's no statute of limitations on murder," he said simply. "My cousin's an RCMP officer in Sydney. They're willing to reopen the case. Ally, I need to ask this, have you been back to the place where you grew up? The bridge and the church? The graveyard?"

"No, I haven't."

"Maybe it would be a good idea to go back to that graveyard. Take a second look. Go over it again with my cousin. I know what the lawyers argued, that you couldn't have seen or heard what you did from the distance in the graveyard."

"But I did."

"Let's go there and prove it."

"Mark, I can't go to Sydney with you. I have Maddy to think about."

"I was thinking she could come. All three of us could go. It would be for one night. My cousin has this huge house in Sydney. It's an old Victorian place with about a dozen bedrooms. You and Maddy would have your choice of the entire second floor. When I visit, I stay in a room on the main floor. The house is beautiful. And my cousin really wants to help us in this."

"But Maddy has school."

"Well..." I could almost hear the wheels turning. "We could leave after school one day and drive back the next. She would only have to miss one day."

"Or we could wait until the weekend," I suggested.

"So, you're thinking about it?"

"I never said that."

"Ally, this is really important, don't you think? You have to trust me. I know Larry Fremont. I know what he's capable of."

Trust you. This early in the morning and I was getting a headache. "This is totally out of the question. I can't go with you to Sydney just like that."

He went on, undaunted. "This is important. Carolyn thinks Larry's responsible for her husband's death. If you come with me to Sydney, maybe we could tie the two cases together." I put my hand on my forehead while Mark continued, "Belle threatened Carolyn."

"What?" I was brought back to the present. "When? At the funeral?"

"No. Carolyn got an unexpected visitor. Belle knocked on her door and basically told her to back off."

I thought about the slightly tipsy Belle.

"Anyway, Ally, promise me you'll think about this. That's all I ask at this point, that you'll just think about it."

When we hung up the phone, I was trembling all over.

EIGHT

The first thing Maddy did when Katie dropped her off after church was to lay down a pair of brand-new ice skates on the kitchen table. Brand-new. Her size. Just the ones she wanted.

"Where did you get those?" I asked her.

She signed. "They used to be Miranda's, but they don't fit her anymore." And then she sat right down on the kitchen floor and pulled them on to show me. There was plenty of room in the toes. I knew they were new. I knew Katie had gone out and bought new skates. My eyes filled with tears, I actually had to look away so my daughter wouldn't see me cry. I told Maddy they were beautiful and wasn't she lucky that Miranda outgrew them?

Over lunch she told me everything they did on the weekend: shopping, ice cream, the library, sledding and skating.

"How did you manage to do all of that in one day?" I asked.

She shrugged, but there was a grin from ear to ear. "I don't know," she signed. "Miranda's mother runs a lot."

I laughed at that and hugged her. That was Katie to a tee: small, determined, a tireless advocate for her daughter, and by default, mine. I told her she couldn't wear her skates in the house and, reluctantly, she took them off. Then she clapped her hands and jumped around the room. Maddy jumps a lot and often in rhythm. I think she likes the vibrations. Like television watching, this is another thing I don't mind her doing.

In the evening we cuddled together on the couch for a while, and I smoothed her curly strawberry hair between my fingers. I held her for a long time, wishing that she could go through life unscathed. I wished for her dreams that were always pure.

Later in her bed she signed, "Can we go to the zoo tomorrow?"

"It's kind of cold for the zoo, don't you think? And tomorrow you have school."

"Or maybe skating then?"

"Skating it will be, then," I said.

"With my new skates."

"Your new skates."

"Can you read me a book?"

"Sure thing. Which book would you like?"

"Dragonrider."

I snuggled onto the bed with her and I read to her, signing in front of her, which is how I read to her. I did this until she fell asleep in my arms.

Long after Maddy had gone to bed that night there came a knock on my front door.

I got up uncertainly. I don't have one of those little peepholes, but I do have a narrow window beside my door. I opened the curtain and peered through it.

Belle Fremont, Larry's wife, stood there in a long beige coat, a blue scarf wrapped around her head and neck and up over her chin. One hand clenched at her stomach. Even from this distance, her eyes looked drooped and tired.

I opened my door a crack.

"Belle?" I said.

"May I come in?"

"What are you doing here?"

"I need to talk to you. It's important. It's really important." She sounded on the verge of tears.

I opened the door. She moved past me quickly and as she did so I caught a whiff of some expensive scent. Mark told me she had paid a visit to Carolyn. Was she here to tell me the same thing, to back off?

She stood in my hallway and pulled off her leather gloves one finger at a time. Her fingers shook as she did so. Without saying anything she walked past me and into my living room and sat down on the couch. I followed her in and sat across from her. She reached over and touched Maddy's framed school picture. "You are so fortunate to have such a beautiful daughter. Lawrence and I were never able to have children."

Lawrence? She called him Lawrence?

The scarf, which looked cashmere, slipped down a bit off her chin and I caught a glimpse of a dark blue bruise on her lower jaw. When she saw where I was looking, she quickly pulled the scarf back up to hide it.

"I fell. Getting into my car," she explained. "I stumbled and my face landed on the steering wheel."

I looked at her and tried to equate this picture with the self-confident Belle I remembered from my childhood. I remembered the way she would try to lord it over us, the painful things she would say. "Tracy only wants to be your friend because your dad gets her free candy."

"That's not true!" I'd yelled at her.

"You're such a creep," she would retort.

I looked at her now and thought about the placement of the bruise on her jaw. You would have to fall very oddly to injure that particular spot. That kind of bruise could have come from only one place. It wasn't there yesterday at the funeral. I thought of the way she seemed to cringe from Larry. Had my presence there cause a repercussion all the way down the line?

I told her how sorry I was. For her fall.

There were dark circles under both of her eyes.

"You're probably wondering why I'm here," she said.

I nodded. "That thought did cross my mind. Especially because it's almost midnight."

She glanced up at the clock on my wall. "It's that late? I didn't mean to come this late. I've been driving around. Had no idea of the time...."

I didn't say anything.

She looked wildly around her. "I'll need to get back soon." She took a breath. Her eyes welled. "But I need to tell you something. Your appearing at the funeral has left everyone in a tailspin. Especially Mama."

"Mama?" I raised my eyebrows at this sweet little name. "You mean, Eloise?" The very thought of calling Eloise "Mama" seemed ludicrous.

She nodded. "Eloise insists that we all call her Mama."

"How precious."

She glared at me for a minute. Absently, she touched her jaw, moved it a bit, winced a little.

I said, "Is he hurting you?"

She didn't answer me. She said, "You need to leave the whole thing alone. Please."

"What whole thing are you talking about?" I challenged.

"Paul Ashton. His death. It was an accident. It has nothing to do with you."

"Is that why you're here? You think I know something about Paul Ashton's death?"

"Everyone thinks..." She stopped, seemed to need

to catch her breath, then began a different thread. "No one knows why you came to the funeral. That has everyone worried."

"I came as Mark's guest."

"And you are going to say it's just a coincidence that you met Mark?"

A coincidence? "I suppose it is, Belle," I said, not fully understanding her meaning.

She moved her head, which caused her scarf to come askew. She pulled the scarf higher, but as she did so I could see that the bruise was quite extensive.

"Have you had your jaw looked at?" I asked.

"I'm fine." She tied the whole thing under her neck like a babushka.

"Did he hit you because I showed up at the funeral?"

"I told you. I fell when I was getting out of my car."

"You told me it was while you were getting *into* your car. And that you fell against the steering wheel."

"Yes, that's how it was. Why I'm here has nothing to do with the fall I had."

But I wasn't so sure about that. No wonder she drank too much, seemed so afraid. She'd gotten what she wanted; Larry and the Fremont money, but had it been worth the price? I felt sorry for her.

She picked up Maddy's school picture and studied it. "She's such a pretty little girl." She put the picture back. "You want to keep her safe, I presume."

I stared at her, then said the words very evenly, very slowly, "What are you talking about?"

"I'm sure you know by now that the Fremonts have the power to do just about anything in this world. Nothing and no one is out of their grasp. You and that boyfriend of yours and your daughter. You can't be too careful. I'm just warning you. They can do a lot of things. They can make people disappear. They can even make contracts disappear." She picked up her gloves and twisted them between shaky fingers. "And if I were you, I would forget what happened in Cape Breton entirely. Entirely." She rose, buttoned up her coat. "That's all I wanted to say. Just be careful."

I didn't know what to say, so I said nothing. *The Fremonts had taken the boat-building contract away from us?* How could they have accomplished that? Yet I knew in my heart, if you have enough money, you can do just about anything.

"There's something else you need to know. Larry didn't kill Tracy. She was on that bridge because she was going to kill Larry. That was her plan."

"And you know this how?"

"For the simple reason that she told me." She sat down suddenly, groaning and clutching her stomach. She righted herself. "I just want to know, Alicia, does the craziness ever go away?"

"What craziness?"

"I know you had a bout of it after Tracy died, remembering things incorrectly, seeing and hearing things that weren't there…the…" Her breath came out ragged and she was doubled over on my couch. What had that monster done to her?

"Are you okay, Belle? Should I call an ambulance?"

"I'm fine. When I fell…I hurt… My stomach." She was breathing rapidly. "May I used your bathroom?"

I pointed. "Down the hall."

I took the opportunity to quickly check on Maddy, who was sleeping soundly. When I came back downstairs, Belle seemed composed and in control once again. "I need to go now."

"Are you sure you're going to be okay?"

She nodded and ducked out of my house without saying goodbye.

The following morning when I dropped off Maddy at school, I hugged her perhaps a little too fiercely.

"Maddy," I instructed her. "Stay inside the school until I come to pick you up."

"Oh, Mom," she signed.

Be very, very careful, my child. As I watched her run toward the school doors, I hoped she was truly safe here. Should I have kept her home from school for a few days? Should I talk to someone at the school? Or were Belle's admonitions merely the ramblings of a crazy woman?

After she was safely inside, I called Carolyn on my cell. At the funeral she told me she wanted to talk with me. Maybe today would be a good time.

She said, "Why don't you come over right now. I'm still in my pajamas, though. I can't seem to rouse myself to do much of anything these days. But come over. I'll make some coffee." She gave me directions to her house and I pulled over to the side of the road and wrote them down.

I called Rod, told him I would probably not be in today. I needed to make up my mind about going to Sydney before I saw Mark again.

Before I got off the phone he handed it to Jolene who said, "I'm dying today. Can we go for lunch? My mother had to run back to PEI for work and she won't be back until tomorrow. Hopefully little miss won't show her face until my mother gets back."

"I've got an idea," I said. "I'm supposed to see Carolyn Ashton in a little while. Why don't you come along?"

A pause, a hesitation. "Ally, I don't even know her."

"That doesn't matter. She wants to talk with me

about Tracy, about what happened to her. I'm sure she wouldn't mind a visitor."

"I don't know, Ally. I don't know any of those people..."

"I know. But you know the story about Tracy just about better than anyone. And unlike my parents, you actually believe me..."

"Because I know you. Okay. I'll come. If you need moral support."

We made plans and I picked her up twenty minutes later.

Carolyn Ashton lived in a beautiful house on the east side of Halifax in a community of large, new homes. She met us at the door in sweatpants and an oversized gray sweatshirt. I wondered if it had belonged to her husband. If she was surprised that I'd brought along a friend, she didn't say anything.

"Come in," she said to the two of us. Her smile was friendly, although she looked tired. "I'm just getting some coffee. I'm glad you could come over. Mark said you might be able to help me."

"Carolyn, this is my friend Jolene. I hope you don't mind that I brought her along. She knows everything there is to know about Larry."

"It's nice to meet you, Jolene." She extended her hand. "Let me get some coffee. Why don't both of you come in?"

"Don't go to any trouble," I said.

"It's no trouble. I could use some anyway. Maybe it'll wake me up."

We followed her through a wide hallway to her kitchen. The house was a beautiful place, all done up in vibrant colors. As we passed the living room I saw what looked like Persian carpets on the hardwood floor. In the background we heard soft Christian music, the kind that had been played at her husband's memorial service.

She said to me, "You must know, then, how close our families were. John and Leah and Paul and I have been friends for a long time. Our kids grew up together. It will be so strange without..." She didn't go on.

I thought about the way the eldest daughter clung to Mark. Then chided myself for such a thought at this time.

"He died a week and a half ago," she said. "I can't believe so many days have passed without him. I keep expecting him to walk through that door, pulling his suitcase behind him, home from a business trip. It can't be that he won't ever come back. It can't be."

Jolene put her hand on the woman's arm. "I am so sorry."

The counters of her kitchen were spread with containers of food, muffins, cakes, squares, loaves of bread. She set the coffeepot to brew and invited us to sit at the kitchen table. "If you're hungry I have tons of food. People just keep bringing it over."

Jolene said, "People bring food because you mean so much to them."

For all of Jolene's balking at visiting a grieving person she didn't know, she was handling the whole thing with grace and ease. Not like me, who felt my eyes tear up at every turn. All I could do was think about Tracy.

Carolyn placed a tinfoil plate of tiny cinnamon buns out on her kitchen table. "These are cinnamon swirls. My children tell me these are very good." She picked up one, took a bite and put it down. "I can't eat anything." Then she turned to me. "I'm so glad Mark has finally found someone." She smiled a bit at me. "He's been a confirmed bachelor for such a long time, we never thought he'd find someone. We've been praying that he would find a nice Christian girl. It looks like our prayers have been answered."

I felt my mouth go dry.

She got up and got coffee mugs down from a cupboard. "Tell me, what church do you go to?"

I choked a bit. Jolene regarded me wryly. "Um," I tried to change the subject. "Mark said you wanted to talk with me?"

"Yes." She turned and ran her fingers through her short, curly hair. "I guess I'm just looking for information. I'm sure that my husband's death was not…" She paused. "Was not accidental. I'm sure Larry knows something."

"I agree with you."

The coffee was ready and she poured three cups. She didn't offer any cream or sugar. She was distracted, I figured, and so not wanting to bother her with this I took a sip of it black. Jolene, who was shunning all caffeine products now that she was pregnant, let hers sit in front of her.

Carolyn seemed not to notice that Jolene wasn't drinking. She played with her fingers in her lap. "I mean, I try to trust God in all of this, but I feel like David. I'm up to my neck in the mire and I can't get out. It's like I'm in quicksand."

"It's been only a week and a half," I said. "It will take more time than that."

She nodded. "I suppose. I just…" She looked around and her eyes filled with tears. "I just want him back."

I nodded. "I know."

"I had a visit from Belle Fremont," she said.

"So did I," I said taking a sip of my black coffee. It was good this way. "What did she say to you?" I asked.

"She came, conveying the sympathies from the family, but she came by herself. She looked a mess, I might add. Her hair was all over the place and didn't look like she'd even combed it. Although I should talk these days." She paused and went on. "She said she was sorry about the tragic accident and warned me not to analyze it too much, just to accept it. She told me that it could make me crazy and it does no good. I'm trying to quote her word for word. But her message was clear, back off. John warned Paul not to go to work for Lawrence." She was still talking. It was like all the pent-up thoughts and feelings were coming out.

"I've been looking through Paul's computer," she went on. "I can't find anything on Fremont Enterprises. Just a few e-mails back and forth with a subject line called the Zacchaeus Plan."

Zacchaeus Plan? It had been a whole lot of years since I'd been to Sunday School, but the only Zacchaeus I knew about was a little man who climbed up a sycamore tree to see Jesus. I asked. "Do you know what that's about?"

She shook her head. "Not a clue."

"What did the e-mails say?"

She rose. "I'll get them. Maybe you can make sense of them. Paul's records for those three months were all on his flash drive. And that wasn't among his belongings that were returned to me from the hotel where he...died."

"Did he usually have his flash drive with him?" I asked.

She nodded. "On his keychain. And it's weird because it looked as if his computer had been tampered with. All recent e-mails were deleted."

"Where did you get the Zacchaeus Plan ones, then?" Jolene asked. She was leaning forward on the kitchen table her head in one hand, listening intently.

She put her hands around her coffee cup. "He used to archive his e-mails. He would change them all to

RTFs and stick them in a text file. I knew this, but if you didn't know where to look, you wouldn't find them. Here, I'll go get them. I've printed them off."

When she left, Jolene turned to me. "She thinks you're a little P.I."

I shook my head. "I don't know how I can help, though."

She returned with two printed pages of back-and-forth e-mails and set them down on the table in front of me. I picked up the first sheet. The subject line was The Zacchaeus Plan. And it was from Paul to Larry. I read, "I'm getting it implemented for you per the attached file."

I looked at Carolyn. "Do you have the attached file?"

She shook her head. "I've looked everywhere on his computer. I can't find that."

There was another page of e-mails listing the times and places of their meetings in Portland, and then a final e-mail from Larry to Paul. "And you are aware of the secrecy of this plan."

"And you have no idea what this Zacchaeus Plan is?" I asked.

She shook her head. "None."

"Have you talked to the police about it?"

"Yes. They don't think it means anything."

I wasn't sure whether I should, either. If it didn't raise any red flags with the police, then perhaps it shouldn't with me. But then I remembered the ineptness of the police when it came to Tracy's investigation. There was nothing substantial in any of these e-mails. I laid them back down on the table, and Jolene picked them up and began to peruse them.

Carolyn leaned toward me and said, "I have no idea what Paul was involved in, but the fact that it was secret bothers me." She paused. "Do you think Larry could, um, kill someone?"

"I do," I said with conviction. I decided to tell her and spent the next fifteen minutes relaying my story.

When I was finished she put her hand on mine. "What a horrible thing to go through."

I nodded.

"A person doesn't forget something like that."

"You're right."

"God must've really helped you through this and to the point where you can even talk about it. I feel so weak, especially in dealing with people like the Fremonts. How have you gotten through it?"

I haven't, I wanted to say. The wounds were still as raw as they were twenty-five years ago. I merely shrugged and looked down at my hands. We talked for a little while longer. I decided not to take the printout of Paul's e-mails with me. There wasn't much there other than the references to the Zacchaeus Plan.

Before we left, Carolyn said, "Would you mind if we prayed before you go? It would mean so much to me."

When she bowed her head and started with, "Dear God," Jolene shot me a glance. As I bowed my head, I said to myself it was out of respect and nothing else. I wasn't praying—surely not. She asked God if she was doing the right thing and if she wasn't that God would stop her. And then she prayed that God would comfort her children. As we stayed in prayer around her kitchen table, something began to soften in my soul, some long-dead thing, some hard place. Maybe there was a God who cared. Would God help me? Did He love me? Had He loved me all along? Could I know?

Our heads were still bowed when she finished. It was obvious that Carolyn expected us to pray in turn, but the moment was cut short by the jingle of a phone in the next room.

Carolyn said to us, "I have to get that."

Jolene and I stayed in her kitchen while she left to answer it. I couldn't hear much. The only thing was the occasional, "Okay, then, I'll tell the family. Thank you very much."

Her voice became quiet. She was gone a long time. Jolene and I didn't know whether we should leave or stay. We decided to stay.

She came out, holding her cell phone. Her eyes darted from Jolene to me, back to Jolene. Her voice was raspy and she had to swallow several times before she said, "They've just released the body. Though the results are inconclusive, they're saying it looks like murder."

"Of course we know it was murder," Jolene said to me when we were in the car and on the way home from Carolyn's. "And we know who did it, even if the police don't."

I nodded, while I looked straight ahead of me on the road.

"From all that you've told me about Larry Fremont, I really believe he had more to do with this than anyone might think. I've been reading the papers, too, Ally. I'm glad I was able to come along to meet Carolyn." She placed her hand across her belly and winced, ever so slightly. "I'm glad you made me come. I didn't want to, you know."

"I know."

Her wincing increased. "Are you okay?" I asked.

"Oh, man!" she said as I stopped slowly at a red light, so we wouldn't skid along the snow.

"Oh, man, what?"

"This baby's going to be a soccer player that's for sure," she said.

"Kicking hard?" I asked.

"She's going to be on the women's Olympic soccer team. I should sign her up right now."

I gripped the steering wheel and asked, "Will she be born this weekend, do you think?" I stared straight ahead. "I don't want to miss it."

"What's happening on the weekend?"

"I might be going to Sydney with Mark for a couple of days." I still wasn't looking at her.

A silence. A pause. Then a deep chuckle or was that a gasp? "Sydney? With Mark? And you drop this on me all of a sudden. Hello! You don't just casually say, 'I'm going to Sydney with Mark' without some sort of lead-up. Do tell." Then more thoughtfully she said, "I always thought Mark was one of those straight-as-an-arrow guys. You must be quite something to get him to whisk you off to Sydney for a romantic weekend."

"No, no. It's nothing like that. It's not a romantic trip. We're just friends. It's a business trip. Well, more like a 'get Larry' trip. And Maddy's coming. Mark has a cousin who's a cop. We'll be going to see him about Tracy. Staying at some big house he owns. They're re-opening the case."

"A cop cousin. I wonder if he's as good looking as Mark?"

"I guess I'll find out."

NINE

As soon as I walked in the door, before I'd even taken off my jacket, I called Mark.

"I'd like to go to Sydney," I told him. "This weekend. I don't want to take Maddy out of school. Now that we know for sure Paul was murdered. I'm glad that your cousin wants to reopen the case."

"You will? You'll go?" I wanted to interpret the eagerness in his voice as anticipation of seeing me, rather than proving that the man who had ruined his business had also killed two people. Maybe it was a little of both, but as we talked, I realized how much I was looking forward to seeing him. Maybe on the drive up to Sydney he would open up and tell me all about his business. Maybe I could encourage him to try again. Maybe I could find out if he was, in fact, related to the famous Longstreets.

We talked about the fact that this was now a murder—"maybe" a murder, he corrected me. "They're saying it's inconclusive," he said.

"Do you believe that?"

"No," he said. "Has Eloise tried calling you again?"

"No," I said. "Every time I come home, I check the phone, and there hasn't been a message from her. Perhaps she's given up on me."

"If she does call again, maybe you should see her."

"Really?"

"Find out what she wants. It might help."

I promised I would.

We made arrangements to leave Saturday morning. His cousin would meet us on the highway and we would drive over to my little town together. "Are you up for that?" he asked.

"I guess."

"We'll be with you."

"Thanks. And, Mark?"

"Yeah?"

"Thanks for taking such an interest in this. I know Tracy was murdered. I know Larry pushed her off. I don't want Carolyn to go through the rest of her life like me, knowing something to be true, yet not being able to prove it. Thank your cousin for me for opening up the case again. It's a relief to have someone finally believe me."

"I believe you," he said.

"Thank you."

"You're a special person, Ally."

What did that mean? I hung up the phone and leaned against my counter and closed my eyes. No, I chided myself, you're letting your feelings run away with you. You and Mark are merely colleagues.

Moments later the phone rang. Mark, again? Maybe he forgot something. Eagerly, I answered it before the end of the first ring.

"Alicia?" I immediately recognized her voice. "This is Eloise Fremont."

"Yes."

"It's vital that I meet with you. Are you available today?"

"Today?" I clutched at the phone.

"Yes, today. I will give you the address to my apartment. Can you be here in an hour? I can't stress how important this is."

I thought about what Mark said, that maybe I should meet with her. I grabbed a piece of paper and jotted down her address and told her I'd be there soon.

At one-thirty I wended my way through the streets of Halifax to the waterfront condo where Eloise lived. I took several wrong turns, despite the map I'd printed from the Internet and placed on the seat beside me. I pulled up to the front of the building and wondered where to park in this great sea of BMWs and Mercedes. I saw signs that indicated visitor parking, so I pulled my car to a stop there. Hers was the very top floor. The penthouse. Why was I not surprised? A suited doorman asked if Mrs. Fremont was expecting me.

"Yes," I said. I'm sure he wondered at my jeans, boots and ratty jacket. He wrote my name in a book and accompanied me in the elevator to the top floor. We said nothing to each other on the trip up. As we neared her floor, I found myself becoming increasingly nervous. All I could think about was the Eloise who'd come strutting toward me when I was thirteen, fire in her eyes when I'd dared accuse her son of murder.

I expected maybe a maid to answer the bell chime, but it was Eloise herself who let me in. She appeared to be alone in the condo, which was all done up in pastels, peaches and greens. It was magnificently furnished.

"Come in," she said, but her voice wasn't at all friendly. I followed her to a plant-filled solarium with a round wrought iron table with two chairs. On the table was a gaudy floral teapot and two delicate tiny teacups in saucers. They almost looked like a child's set. She poured tea in both cups and set one in front of me.

"I saw you drinking tea at the funeral. I figured you liked it."

A cup of tea was the last thing I wanted right about now. Fear was making me nauseated.

"Sit down and we can talk," she said.

I did so. She sat across from me.

She wore what looked like lounge pajamas, silky and flouncy which matched her walls. If not for her heavily jowled face, she would have blended in with the walls. "You need to keep away from my son," she said abruptly.

"Excuse me?"

"Larry. My son. You need to leave it all alone." She leaned toward me, her face inches from mine. I backed away slightly.

She shook her head. "Dangerous things. Things you don't know about, things you can't know about." She kept rubbing her gnarled knuckles.

I asked, "Are you talking about Paul Ashton's murder or are you talking about Tracy's? Or maybe you mean what Larry did to Mark Bishop."

Her eyes narrowed and she peered at me intently. "How do you know about that? Well, of course you would. You and Mark teamed up as you are."

There was that phrase again. She said, "Quite a coincidence I should think, that he would be the one person you would choose to be with."

Coincidence? I didn't think so. If you stood in the middle of Halifax and swung a cat, you'd hit half a dozen people the Fremonts had defrauded. Although she was leaning painfully close to me, I stood my ground and said evenly, "Why was it so imperative that I come to meet you here in person? You could have told me to leave Larry alone over the phone. I didn't need to traipse all the way down here."

"Yes, you did." Her fingers crooked as tree branches were suddenly stilled, she shoved back her chair and rose. "I need to show you something."

She got up.

I sat in the solarium and looked out at the view of Halifax. This room had a large glass door which gave out onto a deck. I imagined that this entire room was opened up in the summer and the plants flourished.

She was back shortly with a small wooden box, which I thought I recognized. She set it down in front of me on the table.

"What is it?" I asked, although I was beginning to remember. I looked down at it. It couldn't be, I thought.

"Open it," she demanded.

Carefully, I pried off the decorative wooden cover. Nestled there in a bed of old cotton was Tracy's locket—the matching one to my own.

"Where did you get this?"

"I kept it all this time. Larry asked me to."

A souvenir, I thought. Killers keep souvenirs of their victims. "Why are you showing this to me?"

"Larry gave it to me right after Tracy died. A few weeks ago it went missing." Her voice was raspy and she wheezed out each sentence. "The last time I was at Belle's house I did a bit of searching through her things. I found it in her jewelry box. When I confronted her about taking it from my house, she denied it."

I was confused. "Why would she take this? And why would Larry care?"

I picked up the locket and opened it, expecting to see the picture of Tracy and me that we'd taken in the photo booth in a Sydney mall. Instead, there was a picture of a sixteen-year-old Larry. I blinked.

She said, "That girl was infatuated with Larry. I

thought if you saw this, you would understand. I'm showing this to you because I need you to leave Larry alone. He kept it all these years. That's how much he thought of Tracy. He would never have killed her. I think he was in love with her. You need to just leave it alone."

"Funny," I said. "Belle came to my house and told me the same thing."

"Belle…" Her eyes darted around the room. "That woman…" But she didn't go on.

"He's abusing her, isn't he?"

She stopped, stared at me.

"Larry. He's hitting her, right? Maybe that's why she stole the locket from you. I saw the bruise on her chin. Is he abusing you, too? Is that why you wanted me to leave it alone? Are you worried that he'll kill you?"

She pushed her chair back so suddenly that a cat I hadn't noticed before yowled loudly and ran down a hall. She coughed several times.

I said, "Well, maybe you're abusing her, then. Because sure as anything, someone is."

Her fingers shook as she placed the locket back in the wooden box. She turned slowly and her eyes met mine. "I'm on your side, Alicia. I know you're not going to believe me, but I'm on your side. And…and, you don't know what you're dealing with. Just stay away from my family."

When I didn't say anything, she added, "I'm prepared to offer you money."

I stared at her, not quite comprehending what she had just said.

Her voice grew fainter. "I know all about Maddy, about the financial difficulties you've had lately. I know that money would help you."

I looked at her fleshy face and hated her for the instant

or two when I wanted to take her money. I needed it. I could use it. And she knew that. But I knew that if I said yes, if I took her money, any bit of it, something inside of me would break and would never be whole again.

"I don't want your money," I spat out.

"Think of Maddy. It's the least we can do."

"Leave my daughter out of this. You will have nothing to do with her."

"Please..." And she reached forward and tried to grasp my hand. I pulled away. "Take the money. Leave us alone."

I pushed back my chair, grabbed my coat and let myself out of the apartment.

On the way out something caught my eye. Belle's blue scarf, the one she'd worn to cover her bruises when she'd come to see me, was draped along the back of a chair in the hall.

TEN

Prior to our leaving, I bought extra newspapers and read every article I possibly could find about the murder of Paul Ashton—because that's what everyone was calling it now. Murder. In bold letters. On the front page. The authorities were now examining Larry's books, and his finances were now under the scrutinizing glare of the media, as they always are when these sorts of things happen.

Had Larry hired someone to get rid of Ashton when he found discrepancies in the Fremont books? Because Larry's whereabouts had been accounted for during every moment of the night Ashton died, that was certainly becoming the favored theory.

I'd seen Carolyn on the local news surrounded by her family, saying that she hoped justice would be done. Next up was Larry Fremont standing bold and large in the lights of the TV camera like he was well used to them.

"My books," he said, spreading his palms wide in a theatrical gesture, "are open. I've lived my life in the public light. I've nothing to hide. We are dedicated to finding the perpetrator of this awful crime. And although he had worked for me only a few months, Paul was like a brother to me."

Right, I thought, and if you believe that, I've got a bridge for sale.

When I told Maddy we were going to Sydney with Mark, she burst into smiles. She's her mother's daughter and likes adventure. She immediately got out her pink suitcase and the first things in were her new skates. When I told this to Mark, he said, "I meant to mention that. If you have skates bring them, too. There's a small pond on the property. Maybe we'll have time to go skating."

A small pond on the property? What kind of a house did his cousin live in? I dug around in the basement until I found my own skates. Maddy insisted on taking Curly Duck, a fluffy yellow duck my parents had given her for Easter two years ago.

I stood my ground when she began packing her whole pony collection.

"No," I signed. "We're going for only one night. You may take three ponies." I put up three fingers.

She put up six.

I put up three.

She put up five.

I put up three.

My daughter is quite the little negotiator.

But if Maddy was having difficulty packing, I was having a worse time. Jolene arrived when I was in the thick of it.

"Shouldn't you be at home and not gallivanting around the neighborhood?" I told her.

"I'll die of boredom if I don't do things. My mother comes back day after tomorrow. Did you know that there are cultures where pregnant women work out in the fields? Then they duck behind a tree, have their babies, strap their little ones on their backs and are out in the fields working after coffee break."

"Sounds like you," I said.

But she was rooting through my closet. "So what are you taking in terms of clothing on this romantic getaway?"

"Jeans, maybe. A warm sweater. It's not a romantic getaway." But I sat down heavily on my bed, clutching a handful of the sweaters I was trying to decide among. "But I still don't know what to take."

She sat beside me. "You like him, don't you?"

I nodded miserably. "I think so. I mean, we really click. But this is all business for him, I'm afraid. Crime business, but business just the same."

"He likes you, Ally. Anyone with half a brain can see that. Rod thinks so, too."

"Really?" Here I was, in my late thirties and looking to my best friend for confirmation.

She nodded. "Wear your black jeans, pack your dark blue pants."

"Because it's only one night I thought I'd wear the same jeans the next day."

"Oh, my dear, no, you may not do that. You need two pairs of pants. What if you spill coffee on them or something?"

"How often do I spill coffee on my clothes? Don't answer that."

In the end I got my way, I'd wear my black jeans both days, but I'd take a different sweater for the next day. Two sweaters, a baby blue cashmere, which was casual but dressy. I'd gotten it at Value Village, a fact of which I was inexorably proud.

"Soft," Jolene said, picking it up and petting it like a cat. "Huggable."

"Huggable," I said. "Just what I need." But even as I said this, I thought about hugging Mark. "We *did* hold hands. Once." I told her.

"Well, there you go!"

But I could reason that away, too. He had taken my hand because it was too icy for walking. I sighed, folded my blue cashmere sweater and placed it in the bottom of my small carry case. "Just one thing—you're not to have that baby while I'm gone."

"I shall give her strict instructions."

As the day of our departure drew nearer, I began to have second thoughts. What would be gained by going to my childhood home, driving by my old house, going to the footbridge and standing there and reliving it? What would be gained by reopening the case? What made me think this time would make any difference after so much time had passed?

In no time at all, it was early morning of the day we were to leave and Mark was pulling up into our driveway. We loaded our few bags and as we got in and I fastened my seat belt, I wondered for the umpteenth time why I was getting in a car with this man and driving off to some strange relative's.

The day was cold and clear, and for all of Maddy's excited signing and smiles, she was asleep in the backseat before we were even on the highway out of Halifax.

Our talk was small and was mostly about the weather and the storm. I said, "Tell me about your cousin's skating pond? What kind of house has a skating pond attached to it?"

"It's the house my mother grew up in. My mother's sister raised her family there. We lived in another house in the area and moved to Halifax when I was sixteen. I'm an only child, so my cousin and I are close."

"Is that the famous Longstreet family?" I asked.

"Yep. The very ones." He eyed me.

"What about your aunt?"

"She spends her winters in Florida. She's there now. So, it's just my cousin in the house. I try to visit as often as I can."

A little while later, I said, "I'm a little nervous about going back there. I don't know how I'm going to feel."

"You'll do fine."

"I hope." I looked down at my hands, which were folded, tightly in my lap. Outside, white winter scenery flew by.

I turned around and looked into the backseat. Maddy was still asleep, clutching Curly Duck. I turned back to the front and said, "Sometimes I wonder if I even remembered it correctly." I paused. "I have these dreams where I remember everything all different. Sometimes I'm there and it's his father who pushes Tracy off. And then in the next dream it's his mother who pushes her off."

He interrupted me. "She is quite the character, isn't she? His mother, I mean."

"You got that right."

He said, "Maybe when you look at all of that again, it will jog something in your memory. And my cousin will be there to help."

"Either that or I'll be more confused than ever."

"I've been praying that all of it will become clear to you. That we'll finally find an end to the mystery."

"Thank you," I said. "I have trouble believing in my own prayers, so it's nice when someone else can pray."

"And speaking of prayer," he said. "Carolyn said it meant a lot to her when you and Jolene visited her. She said you all prayed at the end."

I sighed. "I wouldn't say that. She prayed and we just sort of sat there. I don't think God hears the prayers of reprobates much anyway."

He looked ahead as we passed a car. "You'd be surprised. I think God hears the prayers of the reprobate all the time."

I didn't answer him as the mile markers sped by us.

Finally I said. "Maybe it's not so much that I don't believe in God as it's I'm still quite angry with God."

"For what?"

I turned and faced him square on, open mouthed. "For *what?* For killing my best friend and destroying my family. Haven't you heard anything I've told you about my wretched life?"

"Your wretched life? Look at you. You're healthy. So you had a bad marriage, but look what you got out of it? A wonderful daughter. You live in a great, little funky town house. You're smart, extremely talented. And from what you've told me your parents are quite happy on PEI. Your dad has a better and bigger pharmacy than the one he owned when you grew up. I'd say getting out of there was a good thing. You have a lot going for you. Plus, you're pretty. I say you've done very well for yourself…."

Plus, you're *pretty?*

I said, "I bet you've never been mad at God in your whole life."

"You'd be surprised."

"That business you started, the one where Larry bailed."

His expression darkened. He turned his attention back to the road and didn't say anything for a while. "Yes," he said grimly. "I would say that qualifies."

"But you got over it."

It was a long time before he said, "I'm still working on it. Maybe I want him brought to justice as much as you do." I thought I heard him add, "Maybe more," but I wasn't sure. "Meeting with my cousin, going over all of this again. Maybe it'll help."

"You keep saying 'my cousin.' Does your cousin have a name? Is he like you? You grew up like brothers, you said."

He looked over at me and raised his eyebrows. "What did you say?"

"I asked if he has a name."

"I think Thea would find that amusing."

I blinked at him. "Who's Thea?"

"My cousin's name is Thea."

"What kind of a name for a guy is Thea?"

"Probably not a very good name at all. My cousin's not a guy."

"Your cousin is female?"

"Yep. Didn't I tell you that?"

I tried to remember. Had he ever used the "she" pronoun when talking about his cousin? I shook my head. "No. I don't think you ever did. Well," I said, smiling at him, "I look forward to meeting her."

"And *she*—" he emphasized the word "—looks forward to meeting you."

As we neared the Canso Canal, I placed a hand on my jittery stomach. I thought about what Mark had said, how I had made something of my life and did have a lot of things going for me. Maybe if I thought about all the good things, I wouldn't dread going back so much.

Maddy was awake now, and when I turned back, she signed that she wanted to stop for a bathroom break.

"It's probably time we all took a bit of a stretch," Mark said. We pulled over at the next rest stop where we bought gas, coffees, a chocolate milk for Maddy and a bag of doughnut bits and off we were again. Only two hours to go. Maddy asked where we were and I told her. She asked if she'd ever been here before and I said no.

While Maddy played with her ponies, I asked Mark about himself. "I hope you don't think I'm being too personal, but how is it that a guy like you never married?"

"Never found the right woman, I suppose…" He stopped and there was a look in his eyes I couldn't read. I didn't pursue it. A little while later he said, "You'll have to direct me. Do you know the gas station where we'll be meeting Thea? It's right at the exit for your town."

"I believe it's just up ahead."

In the backseat, Maddy was finishing up her chocolate milk. And as I watched her, slurping up the last of the milk with her straw, I realized that I had put this off far too long. I needed to do this for her. She deserved more of me than I was giving. She deserved a mother who wasn't afraid, wasn't bitter. And wasn't mad at God.

ELEVEN

Several cars were idling in the cold parking lot where we were to meet Thea, and Mark said, "She's not here yet. She has a tendency to be late."

"What are we doing, Mommy?" Maddy signed it from the backseat. "Are we getting out here?"

"Meeting Mark's cousin. Then we're going for a drive."

Maddy and I decided to head into the station for a bathroom break, while Mark filled up with gas. The station was warm and brightly lit and inside it smelled of coffee. I almost succumbed and bought a cup, but I was feeling jittery enough as it was, so I decided against it.

When Maddy and I emerged, Mark was talking to a woman about his age and who matched him in height. She was slender with short, light hair brushed back. She wore jeans, boots and a leather flak jacket.

Hand in hand and with maybe a bit more trepidation that I'd hoped for, Maddy and I approached the two of them.

When Mark saw us coming, he said, "Ally, Maddy, come meet my cousin."

"It's nice to meet you," Thea said.

Her smile was warm and she put me immediately at ease. Like Mark had done, she bent down to Maddy's level and for quite a while they carried on a conversation with me interpreting and Thea doing some rudimentary signs.

When she rose she said to me quietly and confidentially, "Mark told me where we're going today. I want you to know this is a very brave thing you are doing. I've had a look at the old case. There were some questions there that were never answered."

"Like what?"

"The Fremonts' lawyer said you couldn't have seen what you saw."

"But that's not true."

A look passed between Thea and Mark, something that I couldn't read.

"That's what we want to find out," Thea said.

We decided that Thea would ride in Mark's car to town in the backseat with Maddy. Even though their conversation was limited, when I looked back Thea and Maddy were engaged in a sort of conversation, Thea admiring Curly Duck and her ponies.

As we got nearer to my town, familiar scenery rose to meet me. It was an odd feeling, surreal. Things were the way I remembered, yet at the same time, hugely different. Large, modern homes, roadside cafés and gas stations had sprung up, yet I recognized many of the last names on the gas stations and on the mailboxes. Go to any Cape Breton town and certain last names will crop up over and over.

I wondered, casually, how many of these people would remember my name, my parents; probably more than I would care to think about. My name would be coupled with the words "liar" and "storyteller," "the poor family who had to leave because the daughter had all those problems."

People in small towns have long memories and as I

got nearer I began to feel a tingling nervousness. Maddy tapped my shoulder.

I turned.

"Is this where you lived when you were little like me?" she signed.

"Yes," I signed. "When I was little like you, I lived here with Grandma and Grandpa Seward."

"How come we never came here before?" she asked.

"Because Grandma and Grandpa don't live here anymore." I spoke and signed at the same time for the benefit of Mark and Thea.

"Can I see your house?" she asked.

"We'll drive by to see if it's still there," I said.

Mark was laughing now. "You two, talking a mile a minute with your hands. I'd like to learn American sign language. Do they have classes for absolute beginners like me?"

"All the time," I said.

Thea surprised me by saying, "I studied a little. In police academy. I know a few of the basics."

"I can tell," I said.

So that was why Maddy and Thea were getting on so famously.

And then, suddenly, we were at the boundaries of the place where I grew up. In about two blocks this road would become Main Street. A few more blocks and we'd arrive at my father's drugstore, and then a mile from that and down a few roads was the subdivision where I lived.

"Just up ahead," I said. "Where we get to the main part of the town, slow down and I'll show you my father's drugstore."

But when we got to that street, the drugstore didn't seem to be there anymore. The facade was entirely different and it was now a shop that sold women's clothing. I pointed this out as Mark drove past slowly.

Bundled people walked through town, young mothers pulling sleds filled with snow-suited children and groceries. I craned my neck, wondering if I would know any of these people. Probably.

After a little while I told him to keep to the right. I pointed out where to turn and where to slow down until there we were, right in front of the house where I grew up.

"That's my house," I told Maddy.

I wasn't prepared for the flood of emotions that greeted me. The house had changed. Saplings had turned into huge fir trees, the siding was new and a different color, the carport had been turned into a garage. Snow was piled all around it. There were no cars in the driveway and the place looked empty.

Thea had a notebook in her lap, I noticed, plus a tiny camera.

"Are we going in?" Maddy signed.

"Someone else lives here," I spoke and signed. I pointed. "See that window around ground level? That was my bedroom. I used to climb out of that window and meet my best friend Tracy."

"You did?" Maddy signed.

"I did. But that's not what you should do," I said smiling. "And that front window, do you see it? We always had this huge Christmas tree there. And the sidewalks are all different, too. You see the light standard at the end of the driveway? My mother used to have a garden around it. She planted daisies, tulips, all sorts of things."

"How come you don't plant flowers?" Maddy signed.

"Why don't I plant flowers? Because your mother hates any outdoor pursuits that involve land. I prefer the water," I said and signed.

She laughed, Mark laughed, Thea laughed and I felt a little bit less afraid around the edges. I told Mark to drive around the block.

"There," I pointed. "That was Tracy's house."

"They still live there," Thea said.

I looked back at her.

"I checked," she said.

Mark slowed in front of the house.

"What are we doing?" I asked.

"I want to talk with them," Thea said, craning her neck. "I wonder…"

Mark stopped the car.

"What are we doing?" I asked again.

"Are we going to visit your friend?" Maddy signed. "Your friend, Tracy…" She finger spelled the name.

I blinked at her, realizing just how impossible it is for me to keep anything from her.

To Mark and Thea I said, "Tracy's parents didn't believe me, either. I think that was the most heartbreaking."

While we were stopped there, a woman came out onto the porch and looked at us. I knew at once that this was Tracy's mother. She wore brown pants and a sloppy pink sweatshirt with writing on the front. Her gray hair was poofed out at the sides and she was squinting at us. When I was a girl, Tracy's mother's hair was brown, but essentially in the same style as today.

Tracy had inherited her mother's curly hair. I remember that she always despised it and used all sorts of straightening irons and gels to change it.

"Maybe this would be a good time to talk with her," Thea said. "I'll take the lead."

I opened my door and got out and helped Maddy out, and the four of us made our way up the walkway toward her.

"Mrs. York?" Thea asked.

"Yes?" It was me she was squinting at.

"My name is Thea Longstreet. I'm with the RCMP in Sydney. Would it be all right if we talked with you for a few minutes?"

She stared at the four of us, and then her eyes fell on Maddy. If she thought it odd that a child should be along at a police questioning, she didn't say anything.

"I…I don't know." She looked confused. She was looking at me now. Finally, it seemed, recognition dawned. "Alicia?" And she backed away, her hand on her mouth.

"Yes. I'm Alicia."

"Tracy's friend?"

I nodded.

She swallowed and said, "After all these years."

"Yes. It has been a long time. This is my daughter, Maddy, and these are my friends, Mark and Thea."

"Oh," was all she said. She kept one hand close to her mouth.

Thea said gently, softly, "May we come in for a few minutes?"

"I suppose. Well, okay. Come in, then."

The four of us followed her inside and into a place that seemed completely unchanged in twenty-five years. The carpet was the one I remembered, the walls were the same color and the furniture seemed shabbier for sure, but the same. It even smelled the way it did back then, like baking bread and cabbage. Whatever Tracy's parents had done in the past twenty-five years, they hadn't spent a lot of time or money on remodeling projects.

The living room floor was old linoleum with a few scatter rugs, the knickknacks on the tables were the same ones I had remembered from my childhood. Tracy's mother led us into the living room and the four of us sat down on a worn couch.

Tracy's father was sprawled onto a recliner chair, asleep, snoring, mouth open. The TV was tuned to a home-makeover program. Before Mrs. York sat down, she went over and kicked his chair. "Wake up, Frank. We have visitors."

He grunted, opened his eyes, closed them, then opened them again and stared at us. At me. If he recognized me, I would be surprised. He'd never paid much attention to me when I was here with Tracy. He was merely a shadowy figure in the background of my childhood who worked all day in the mine and then came home and slept in his chair. And it certainly looked like the same chair. I don't think he said more than three words to me the entire time I knew Tracy.

My gaze shifted around the room and Maddy signed to me. "Is this your friend's mom?"

I signed, "Yes." Mrs. York stared at us.

"My daughter is deaf," I told her. "This is the way we talk with each other."

She nodded and said something about that being too bad. She seemed very nervous.

My eyes locked on the mantel. A framed picture of Tracy was there. She was smiling in her school picture, her face frozen in time. I looked at Mrs. York and new sadness filled my heart.

While Thea open to a page in her small notebook, Tracy's mother surprised me by saying, "Alicia, how is your mother?"

"She's good," I said.

She looked regretful. "We should've kept in touch. Does she have e-mail?"

I wrote my mother's e-mail address on a piece of

paper and handed it to her. I told her that my mother would love to hear from her.

"Your mother was so good to me after the accident. Everything happened and then your parents moved away. I never got a chance to thank your mother."

"I'm sure she knows how you feel."

She bit her lip and looked at me for a long moment. Maddy was swinging her legs and hitting the sofa with the back of them.

"So many people were kind to us back then," she said. "Your parents. And then the Fremonts. They were especially good to us, the Fremonts were, you know."

I blinked at her. I could feel Mark stiffen. Maddy just kept swinging her legs. I put my hands on Maddy's knees to still them.

"The Fremonts were kind to you?" I asked.

"I remember what you said, Alicia, how it was Larry's fault. But I'm sure you realize by now how wrong your accusations were. Not after everything the Fremonts did for us…."

Frank roused from his chair. "Mother," he said. "Let's not rehash that over and over, okay?"

She turned to him. "I have to, Frank. After all these years, these things. They just don't die, you know." She was still talking. "Coming on twenty-five years this June and I still wonder if there was something I could have done."

Frank turned his face away and clicked up the TV volume with the remote. Outside a heavy truck lumbered by.

I turned to her and said, "That day that she…the day of the accident, um, were you supposed to pick me up after school that day?"

"You?" she stared at me.

"Yes, me. Were you supposed to pick up Tracy and me from school?"

"Why would I do that?"

"I thought you were."

"No. Why would I? I worked every day. I never picked Tracy up from school. She took the bus. The police asked us that same question. A long time ago. I told them the same thing."

She frowned and folded her hands in her lap. The writing on her sweatshirt included a pink ribbon from the Breast Cancer Foundation. It made me wonder if this was another battle she'd fought. I hoped she'd won at least this one. She said, "No matter what people say about the Fremonts, they were helpful and generous at the time of Tracy's accident."

She opened her eyes wide and looked at me. "They paid for the entire funeral, did you know that? Frank worked in their mine, but the Fremonts certainly didn't have to do that. They told us it was the least they could do for one of their employees."

She went on, "Every year on Tracy's birthday they sent us a check for two thousand dollars. They certainly didn't need to do that now, did they? The mother, Eloise, she was the one who ran the mine, you know. She said it had to do with our loss, and also the fact that they had to close the mine for economic reasons."

I was shocked by this. Mark and Thea seemed just as stunned as I was. Thea asked, "How did they send you money? Checks?"

She nodded.

"That's not in the police report."

"Why would it be? The Fremonts asked us to keep it quiet. This is something they wanted to do without a lot of people knowing, because of the way the death was. You know."

While Thea continued to question Mrs. York, Mark and I exchanged glances.

Thea asked, "Can you tell us about the accident? What went on that day? What do you remember?"

She did. She started at the beginning. Her voice took on a flat quality as she spoke. I understood that this was a story she'd recited so many times that she had it memorized.

She'd been working day shift at Fay's Diner like she did every day. In the late afternoon she'd looked out and saw the police cars heading up Main Street. Fast. Sirens going. She remembered commenting about this to another waitress. "Must be something serious," she'd said.

The police called her. There'd been an accident. Something to do with Tracy. Could she come to the church right away? The church? She wondered why Tracy would be at the church. The whole way there she wondered. When she got there an officer took her aside and told her that Tracy had somehow fallen from the footbridge. She remembered screaming and saying it wasn't true. It couldn't be true. Not Tracy. Not her only child. She breathed in and said, "They couldn't get Frank right away. He was down five miles in the mine."

I nodded. On the recliner, Frank's eyes were closed, but I doubted that he was asleep.

She continued, "And then you came. With your parents. Your mother…"

I knew what she was thinking. My father had spoken to the police officers. They came and spoke to me. They sat me down and I was crying and crying. Gently, they asked me what I'd seen. I could barely get out my story.

But I did. I told him that Larry had pushed Tracy, that I'd seen everything.

"But that wasn't the way it was. Her death was different."

Thea leaned forward and said, "What do you mean by different?"

Bright patches of red blazed on her cheeks and she touched them with both hands.

Frank reached for the remote clicked off the TV and pulled his recliner into an upright position.

He said, "When she says *different,* it was because it was suicide. We know that Tracy flung herself off that bridge, and that Larry tried to save her in the end."

"Frank!" Mrs. York said.

"Suicide?" The three of us said it together.

Mrs. York nodded slowly. It was a while before she spoke. "She jumped off the bridge. It was all in her diaries and her notes."

"She left a note?" Thea asked. "There was no mention of any note."

She got up and left the room. Thea looked at Mark and Mark looked at Thea and I looked at them both and Maddy asked when are we going? I signed that it wouldn't be long. Frank went back to his home-makeover show.

Mrs. York came back a few minutes later with a small pink diary that I recognized. The keys to the plastic book hung by a dirty string from its lock. For some reason she handed the book to me. I took it, glancing at Thea and Mark as I did so. She said, "You may not take this out of the house. You have to look at it here."

"Let them take it. And after they read it they can burn it." This surprisingly came from Frank.

Mrs. York turned on him. "Frank, I can't let this

book out of the house. I can't let it out of my sight. You know that."

"Alicia needs to understand what happened to Tracy. It's about time you quit holding on to all this stuff with such an iron fist."

Thea said, "It's okay. We can look at it here."

Mrs. York looked confused as she stood over her husband, shaking her head. "Frank, you never should have mentioned the word *suicide.* I never intended for the police to know it was this. I'm only letting you see it, Alicia, because after all these years you need to know that what you thought you saw was incorrect. You need to know the truth."

Lovingly, I ran my hand across the front of the diary. It was the exact match to my own. Like the lockets, we had bought these together. I opened to the first page and I switched places with Maddy so the three of us, Mark, Thea and I could look through the diary.

"You said there was a suicide note?" Thea said.

Mrs. York shook her head. "I never said a suicide note. I said notes written in a diary."

The first page took me back to a year before her death when the two of us were best friends and both happened to be in love with the same boy from camp. She wrote, "He's cute." And I recognized my own writing as I added, "He's really cute." I sighed audibly.

We skimmed through entries about camp and youth group and school. I was aware of Mark sitting close to me. I wondered what he thought about this boy-crazy chapter of my life.

On one page there was a list of all the boys in school ranked with the number of little hearts by their names.

There were a lot of pages with hearts with Larry's name in them. One entry read, *Alicia doesn't think*

Larry's cute. I went to his house and stood outside it and waited there for about an hour. I was hiding in the fields. Alicia told me I was crazy. I don't know why she doesn't want to be my friend anymore. I think it's because of Larry.

I didn't want to be *her* friend?

More of this, more of that and then nearer to the last entry:

Today Larry and I went for a walk across the bridge. I looked down and we talked about what it would be like to fall. It's really far up. I told him I would do that. Belle likes him. She told me so, and if I can't beat Belle, I'm going to kill myself.

I was so mad at Alicia because she called my house and told my father that I was with Larry. And so I got grounded. I'm not old enough to date yet. Which is really stupid. People shouldn't tell on their friends. But then Wanda told me it wasn't true. That Alicia didn't talk to my dad. She knows for sure. So, I don't know who did because my father said it was Alicia who called him on the phone and told him. But I have to see Larry! They just don't understand how much I love him.

I'm going to phone Alicia. I miss her. We used to be such buds.

That was it, the last entry. The rest of the pages were blank.

"Who was this friend who called you, Frank?" Thea said to his sleeping form. "Do you know? Do you remember?"

He opened his eyes and shrugged, looked over at me. "I thought it was you."

I shook my head. There had been a cryptic mention of this in my own diary, but I hadn't understood it. It was hard for me to keep the tears from spilling. I wiped under my eyes with my fingers. Maddy touched my hand. I looked at her.

"What's wrong, Mommy?" she signed.

"I just found out that my best friend was still my best friend, after all," I signed back.

TWELVE

Maddy signed that she wanted a bathroom, so we made our way into the center of town and stopped at a coffee shop that wasn't here when I was little. It was past time for lunch anyway, so we decided on soup and sandwiches. As I was drinking my coffee I kept looking around me, but no one looked familiar and, thankfully no one seemed to recognize me. Kids looked like kids anywhere with their baggy pants, their earphones. I wondered how many of their parents I would know.

We found a table beside the window. I took small bites of my sandwich, but didn't say much. We didn't talk about the book or Tracy or her so-called suicide entry. It was as if by some unspoken agreement we decided that we wouldn't speak of such things in a public place. The only thing I had said was, "Tracy's mother is wrong, you know. If Tracy wanted to reconcile with me, she would never have killed herself. That's how I know it isn't suicide."

At our table, Maddy and I drew a few curious looks with our signing. But we're used to that. After a few moments of watching, most people just go back to whatever it was they were doing before they saw us. Maddy was full of questions about Tracy's parents and

I answered as best I could. She had questions for me, too. She watched us talking and wanted to know what "suicide" was. She finger spelled the word.

How do you explain suicide to an eight-year-old? How do you explain death? "Suicide," I said, finger spelling it, "is when you make yourself have a bad accident."

She thought about that. "You mean, like if I rode my bicycle into a tree on purpose?"

"Something like that. Only a really, really bad accident when you never wake up."

"Like you're dead?" She stroked her finger across her throat and stuck out her tongue, slang for "dead." Even Mark picked up on that one.

"Yes," I signed.

"What happens when you die?"

I paused, my fingers in midair. "You go to sleep for a long, long time."

"Miranda says people can go to Heaven."

Oh, the difficulties of having philosophical discussions like this with children, especially in sign language.

"Maybe they do," I signed. How I wanted to believe that.

Mark said, "What are you two talking about so fast and furiously?"

"Oh, nothing," I said out loud. "Heaven. Death. Suicide. All normal topics of conversation between mother and daughter."

He raised his eyebrows.

"Seriously," I said, my voice quiet so our table neighbors wouldn't hear, "She asked me what suicide was and I explained it to her."

"That's what I thought," Thea said. "I know just enough sign language to be dangerous."

After we left the coffee shop I directed Mark to River

Road. This road held so many memories for me: good ones of bicycling long and hard up the hill so we could coast down, damming up a place in the river with rocks and logs so we'd have an even better swimming hole and then swinging off our favorite rope swing and landing right in the middle of it.

"Up about a quarter of a mile is the church," I said, "You might be able to see the steeple from here. Right over there is the Fremont mansion." It was overblown with snow. It was obvious that no one had been here in quite a while.

"There's the church," I pointed. "Up ahead a bit. You can see it on the right."

"I see it," Thea said. She signed the word *church* to Maddy.

Mark pulled into the church parking lot as if he knew the place.

There were no cars and the lot was neatly plowed. A sign out front indicated when the services were. The graveyard was filled with snow and the grave markers look like bent-over old people making their way through the wild tundra. That's how Tracy and I used to describe them.

I opened my door and Maddy got out and immediately ran to the edge of the graveyard and stepped into the deep snow.

"Maddy!" I called out loud, although she couldn't hear me because she wasn't looking at me. I went to her and stopped for a minute and looked toward the river.

The footbridge was gone. I can't say that I was surprised. One good spring flood and it would've been history. It had been close to happening so often when I was a girl. Also it was a dangerous bridge. The railings were spindly and weak, and were always posted with caution signs.

Mark asked, "Where did the bridge used to be?" Although he seemed to be looking at the exact place.

"Right there," I said. "Where those pilings are."

"I thought so."

"Where were you standing?" Thea asked. She carried her tiny camera in her palm.

"Over here." I trudged over to the graves in heavy, deep snow and pointed. "That grave marker over there, the one next to the tree. It's almost covered with snow, but I remember it because it was black instead of gray."

The three of us trudged through knee-deep snow until we reached it. Maddy thought it was great. She could barely contain her giggles. She began making snow angels, standing up, falling down into the snow and then giggling. And while she did so, I talked through the event with Mark and Thea in every detail.

And although there was no footbridge to stand on, Mark and Thea made their way down to the edge of the water, as near as they could to the place where Tracy had fallen. They talked in raised tones. I heard almost every word. Clearly. Distinctly.

I didn't say much on the way back to pick up Thea's car. Maddy fell asleep almost immediately, and exhausted, I leaned my head against the headrest and closed my eyes and found myself listening to Mark and his cousin. Their voice inflections were similar, and their phrasing, the way they interacted with each other was more like close brother and sister than cousins.

Thea said, "I find the fact that the Fremonts paid for the York funeral very interesting."

"Right," Mark said. "And sending them money."

"None of that was in the police report, none at all," said Thea.

At the gas station. Thea got out and into her own car. We followed her down the highway toward her home.

I didn't say much. I guess I was processing the whole thing. Mark turned on the radio to a quiet contemporary station.

I dozed. I was back at the footbridge. I was looking down at the bug on my ankle and then I heard Tracy's screams. Over and over I heard them. And then Larry's laugh.

I awoke with a jolt when the car stopped. We were at the inner end of a wide circular driveway. Maddy was awake now. Her eyes had turned to saucers and mine did, too.

The house was right on the water and was almost as grand as the Fremont mansion. It was an imposing, white, many-turreted affair with a circular driveway and flags out front. Even though it was a month past Christmas, a large wreath in shades of lavender hung on the front door. In the distance, behind the house, the winter sea roiled, black and tumultuous.

"Wow," was all I could say.

Maddy signed, "Is this a castle?"

Ahead of us, Thea opened the four-car garage and we followed her in. It was empty save for our two cars.

"This place is huge," I said.

"Wait until you see the inside," Mark said. "This house has been in our family a long time."

"Is this where your mother grew up?"

He nodded.

"The Longstreets," I said.

"Right."

We followed Thea through the door in the back of

the garage. The place was enormous and lovely with wide hallways, big furniture and paintings and old hardwood floors.

"It's gorgeous in here," I kept saying.

Thea said, "Welcome to my house. Or more accurately, our family home."

"It's beautiful," I said.

"Members of the family come and go. It's a great vacation spot. I live here by myself in the winter, though."

"Wow. How fortunate you are."

Mark added, "Did you bring your skates?" He turned to his cousin, "Is the skating pond clear?"

"Shoveled it off myself, cuz, because I knew you were coming." She turned to Maddy and me.

"Follow me up the stairs. You two can have your pick of rooms on the second floor. My room is on the main floor and so is Mark's. But we thought you might like to see up there. The view is stunning. I turned the heat on upstairs, this morning before I left for work. So, it should be warm enough."

As we followed her up the wide staircase, our feet barely made a sound on the thick carpet. There were a total of seven bedrooms on the top floor. We ended up choosing a room with two double beds and an adjoining bathroom. The room offered a view of the Atlantic Ocean. Over the water a moon was rising.

Mark yelled up the stairs, "Hey, you guys, you want to go skating? It's beautiful outside. We can skate first and talk business later."

I signed to Maddy, "Do you want to go skating?"

Her eyes lit up. We quickly unpacked and got out our warm skating clothes. Maddy stood by the window and signed, "It's like a fairy tale, like from a book."

"It is," I said. I stood beside her and watched the

water. As if on cue, the outside lights came on, hundreds of little points of light high in the trees shone down on the frozen outdoor pond.

Downstairs, Mark and Thea were waiting. Mark looked so handsome in his green jacket, jeans and black wool toque. He insisted on carrying our skates and led us out through a door in the back of the kitchen, out along a large wooden deck, and down a plowed path to the pond.

"Watch the path," Thea said. "It may be a little icy."

Beside the pond was a long wooden bench where we sat to put on our skates. Maddy kept signing excitedly, until I told her she had to pause long enough to tie up her skates. In the end, Mark knelt in front of her and tied them up for her. I watched him with my daughter and felt a tear at the corner of my eyes. He was so gentle with her, and she was clearly as enamored of him as I was. Was there a chance for the two of us? Since Tracy died, I have felt jinxed and yet I've thought about what Mark said to me. My life really wasn't so bad, was it? And maybe, just maybe, it was about to take a turn for the better.

The four of us held hands and skated in large circles around the pond. The ice surface was smooth and the little blue lights overhead cast dreamlike patterns across the ice surface. The effect was delightful.

Mark said, "When I was a little boy this skating pond was one of my favorite places in the world."

"He wanted to be a hockey player," Thea said.

He chuckled. "I skated every single day after school. I was going to be the next Wayne Gretzky."

"Did you ever play hockey?" I asked.

"Minor hockey. But despite all my practice, I wasn't any good. I ended up quitting and going into competitive sailing, which I was much better at."

"Smart move," I said.

The four of us skated in happy camaraderie for a long time. We chatted about inconsequentials. We remarked on the weather. We looked at the moon.

In a little while, Maddy signed that she was cold and that her legs were tired.

"Why don't you come with me, Maddy?" Thea held out her hand. I interpreted.

"Help me get the pizzas for supper," she said. When I signed the word *pizza,* her eyes lit up.

After they undid their skates, they walked hand in hand up the path toward the house. And Mark and I were left alone. We held hands as we silently skated round and round. I'd been cold when I was helping Maddy unlace her skates, but now the physical exertion of skating well and skating fast was warming me up. Or maybe it was being next to Mark.

He said, "How was it?"

I didn't immediately know what he was referring to. "How was what?"

"Going back there today."

I didn't respond until we were halfway around the pond again. "It wasn't so bad. I don't know what I was afraid of all these years."

"Sometimes confronting fears is a good thing," he said.

"Maybe," I said. We were around once more when I said, "Your cousin is nice. She's a lot like you."

He grinned. "A lot of people say that."

"This is such a beautiful house," I said. "Such lovely grounds."

"It's been in my family a long time. Actually it's the only thing left of the Longstreet mining fortune."

I looked over at him. "What do you mean the only thing left?"

"My family, well, my mother's family lost a lot of money when the mines closed. This house is just about the only thing they managed to salvage."

I slowed my skating, stopped and looked up at him. "I hadn't realized that. All of the people I knew were on the other side of the fence, the miners. I thought all the mine owners came away like bandits."

He shook his head. "Some. Not all. Not us." But he had turned his face away from me and I understood. I remembered the worn ski jacket he used, the frayed sweater. If the Longstreets were wealthy once, they weren't any longer.

A few more turns around the pond and he said, "Thea and Maddy probably have the pizzas ready by now. You want to head up?"

I didn't. I wanted to stay in that fairy-tale place with Mark forever, but I nodded and said, "Pizza sounds good."

When we sat on the bench and took off our skates, I told him again what a beautiful place this was. As we stood up, he moved toward me. "Ally," he said. He reached down and touched my face with his gloved hand. I had the feeling he was going to say something—something about Tracy maybe, and how brave I was for facing my fears head-on. Instead, he repeated my name. "Ally…" Then he placed his hands on the side of my toque and grinning he pulled it down more firmly over my ears. "Don't want you getting cold," he said.

And then his hands were on my cheek and he was pulling me toward him. His lips were warm on my own, and as we stood there, everything else faded, the lights twinkling overhead, the dark sky, even the moon.

When we parted, he said, "I've wanted to do that for a long time."

"You have?"

He nodded. "From the first day I saw you, sitting with your back to me at Maritime Nautical."

He took my hand and the two of us began to make our way up the path to the house. At the doorway I stopped, turned to him. "I just want to thank you for doing this, for taking on my cause. I think it's really helped. It helps knowing that Tracy wanted to reconcile. The trip was worth it just for that."

Maybe it was the shadows or maybe a small cloud had passed in front of the moon or maybe the wind had suddenly moved the lights in the trees, because he let go of my hand and his expression darkened. Just for a moment, hardly a blip, because not an instant later he was smiling and had taken my hand and was telling me that the pizzas were probably ready by now. The whole thing was so sudden that I wondered if I imagined it.

Upstairs Thea was taking the pizzas out of the oven and Maddy was setting the plates on the table. She signed rapidly when the two of us entered. She was teaching Thea signs, she told me, and Thea was a great learner.

And as the four of us shared pizzas in a room with a lit fireplace, I wondered if life could get any better than this.

When it was time to put Maddy into bed, I took her upstairs. Mark said to make sure I came back down again so the three of us could go over the police reports.

"We'll be in the front room by the fireplace," Thea said. "Just follow the voices."

Maddy fell asleep more quickly than I thought. I washed up, combed my hair a bit more, refreshed my makeup and decided to change into the blue cashmere sweater that Jolene had urged me to bring.

My feet didn't make a sound on the carpeted stairs as I made my way quietly toward the fireplace room. I heard the fire crackling and was about to step into the room when I heard Thea say, "And were you able to get a lot of information from her?"

"Sort of," I heard Mark say. "I'm still working on it. She was a bit hazy at the church cemetery, though. I wish she would have been a bit more certain about everything. I think she'll tell us more."

Thea laughed. "She'll tell *you* more in any case, I imagine. You just turn on the charm and the ladies swoon…"

Mark said something I couldn't decipher. I was stopped, unable to move.

Thea said, "Does she seem as unstable to you as the reports seem to indicate?"

I couldn't hear Mark's answer.

A moment later, Thea said, "Do you believe it? The scum actually called me. Wants to meet with me."

"He wants to meet with me, too," Mark said.

"I wonder what business he now has with our family," Thea said. "And you are certainly not going to call him, are you?"

"Thea," Mark hesitated. "I really think we need to give up some of this. I'm thinking maybe I will call him."

I found it hard to equate the friendly, happy Thea that Maddy had gotten along with so well with the voice I was hearing from the room. Thea added, "Quite a coincidence your getting a job in the same place she works."

"It was no coincidence," I heard him say.

There are two things I could have done at that moment. I could've announced myself with wild shrieks of "What are you talking about? How dare you?" Or I could have tiptoed back to the head of the stairs and then made my way noisily down the steps, entering the room as if I'd heard nothing, knew nothing. Mind churning, head pounding and heart breaking, I turned and made my way quietly back up the staircase. I sat down on the top step and put my head in my hands. Bile rose in my throat and for a moment I felt like fleeing into the bathroom and throwing up. I breathed deeply and counted to ten. "God, please help me."

If I had driven here myself, if I had any way out of this castle, I'd pack up Maddy and we'd flee. We'd head out a back door and just run away. I'd drive back to Halifax tonight and I'd forget I ever met anyone named Mark Bishop. Forget he ever kissed me. I put my hand to my mouth. I was shaking all over.

You just turn on the charm and the ladies swoon...

Maddy was still sound asleep when I got back to the room. I shut myself into the bathroom and sat on the toilet seat and bent over, my head into my knees and cried. Mark had gotten to know me, pretended to like me, *kissed* me even, just so he could do what? Get information from me? Why? None of it made any sense.

I washed my face, reapplied my makeup. As I looked at my ghostly reflection in the mirror I decided that I had no choice. I'd have to steel myself, go back down there like nothing happened.

I slammed the door, then thumped loudly down the stairs. I even hummed as I made my way toward the fireplace room. When I entered, the two of them looked up and smiled warmly, brightly at me. I smiled back. He had used me! Why had I stayed away from men all these years? Because they always used me. What else did I expect?

Thea was sitting on the floor, arranging papers and reports and files on the coffee table. Mark was seated at a leather couch. He smiled at me and patted the seat beside him for me to sit on. I didn't. Instead I chose a rather uncomfortable high-backed, floral Victorian chair some distance away.

"You're going to be interested in this," she said. "I managed to photocopy everything. It was ruled an accident. No mention of suicide. Nothing in all these reports about what Mrs. York told us. Nothing about the Fremonts paying for funeral."

I picked up a random piece of paper. Mark said, "You're not going to want to read that."

I read it anyway. It was a psychiatric evaluation of me at age thirteen. It suggested that I had been fueled by jealousy. It suggested that I had made up the entire story.

I put it down and avoided looking at Mark.

"I told you," he said.

Thea said, "Here's where a lawyer tried to prove that you wouldn't be able to see or hear what you said you did from where you stood. He had it all measured out with angles. But we know that quite possibly it could have happened just the way you said it did."

"Well," I said drily, "I'm glad someone believes me."

A log in the fireplace crackled, shifted and sent a shower of sparks. I looked over at it. Suddenly my anger was too much to bear. It was one thing for me to be used by Mark, but it was quite another to realize that Thea had used my daughter. Maddy was a pawn in their plan to bring down Larry. And I wouldn't have that. I squeezed my hands into fists in my lap.

Mark said, "Are you okay, Ally?"

"Just tired I guess. I'm going to turn in. The whole day has been a bit too much for me." I rose stiffly and left the room.

Mark was close at my heels. "Ally? Are you sure you're okay? Is there anything I can get you. Don't you want to read the police report?"

We were at the foot of the stairs.

"If it's that psychiatric report that's bothered you, Ally, I'm sorry, it's nothing but lies, put together by a desperate family."

The report? He thought the report was bothering me?

I was turned and his face was inches from mine. I knew he wanted to kiss me again.

Don't you touch me! I wanted to scream at him. Don't you ever touch me again! I didn't say anything and when he moved his arms around me, I choreographed my way out of them, turned and fled up the stairs to my room. I locked the door behind me and burst into tears on my bed.

THIRTEEN

Monday morning I'd been up since four-thirty rattling around in my kitchen. It was now seven. It was a school day and soon I'd have to wake Maddy, but for now I was alone. Earlier, when I'd determined that I would get no more sleep that night, I'd thrown on some clothes and came downstairs, put in a favorite blues CD and started cleaning out the kitchen cupboards. Cleaning cupboards is good for a broken heart. I should have the cleanest cupboards around, then. If need be, I'd work all day on these cupboards, which were grungier than I imagined. After all, what else was I doing today? Where else was I going? Certainly not to Maritime Nautical where I might bump into Mark.

With my wet sloppy rag I attacked inside the bottom of my pots and pans cupboard. I glanced up at my clock. Still too early to phone Jolene. I needed a good cry with my best friend. So far I hadn't cried much more than a few angry tears in Mark's car.

On the way home yesterday I'd been mostly numb. I was so deeply hurt that I couldn't even look at Mark. During that interminable trip, Mark had looked over at me several times, confused, but I kept my face turned away from him. Because as soon as I would feel myself softening toward him I would remember Thea's words:

You just turn on the charm and the ladies swoon...

Does she seem as unstable to you as the reports seem to indicate?

Two hours into the trip Maddy had fallen asleep and Mark kept his gaze out on the highway when he said, "Ally, something happened last night to change you. If it was..." He paused and moved his hands on the steering wheel. "If I was out of line in kissing you, I apologize."

Hot tears threatened my eyes and I swiped at them. I said nothing.

"Ally?"

"No," I said. That's all I had said, just *no*. I think no was the last word I said to him. It would be the last word I would ever say to him.

I was banging pots, clanging them, really, and the sound was somehow gratifying. And when I looked up Maddy was standing in the door.

"You're making too much noise," she signed.

"I guess I was," I signed back. She could sense the rumbles and thumping.

"You okay?" I asked her.

She nodded. This sudden change had not left her unscathed either. Last night as I was tucking her into bed, she said, "How come you don't like Mark and Thea anymore?" She finger spelled the name Thea.

"I don't dislike them," I said, but even as I smoothed her tangled hair I wondered. Assorted thoughts from my Sunday School days kept emerging into my thinking. Verses about forgiveness, about Christ forgiving us and how we should forgive others. But how was I supposed to forgive Mark? He had used me. And what about

Larry? Was this forgiveness supposed to extend to him? To someone who murdered my best friend?

And now as I held my little daughter in my lap, I thought about forgiveness. It was too late for Mark and me as a couple, but maybe I could at least forgive him and Thea for what they had done to me, if not for their sakes then for mine.

"How about getting ready for school now?" I signed. "Miranda's mom will be here soon."

Maddy jumped down from my lap and ran upstairs to get ready for school.

I sighed and brewed myself a cup of coffee. After Maddy left for school, I'd have another look at the diary.

FOURTEEN

I couldn't find my diary or the locket. They weren't beside my bed. It was the oddest thing. I couldn't remember if I'd seen them when I'd gotten home from Sydney the night before. The only place I had had them was my bedroom and the last place I remembered them being was on my end table there. Maddy had come into my room that morning—had she walked off with them? But why would she?

I had read the diary in my bedroom, nowhere else. I hadn't taken the locket anywhere. I told all this to Jolene when I called her. She was feeling good, she told me. Her mother was back and she was due any day now. When she asked me how my romantic weekend was, I choked.

I brought my feet up underneath me on the couch and told her my sad, miserable story. There would be no more Mark and Ally, and I explained why. "He was using me." I told her.

"Are you sure you heard what you thought you heard?"

Where had I heard that before? "I'm positive." There must've been something in my tone because she said rather quickly, "I'm sorry, Ally. It's just that the Mark I know wouldn't say that."

"The Mark you know.... Let me tell you something about con artists..."

"You need to talk to him," Jolene said. "You need to tell him what you heard and give him a chance to explain."

"A chance to explain? I know what I heard."

I was about to tell her about Mark kissing me when the doorbell rang. My first thought was Mark coming to try to make some sort of amends. I would have none of it.

"Jolene? I've got to go. There's someone at my door. Maybe it's Mark."

"Good. You need to talk to him. Because I can't believe he would say that. You forget, I'm the one who reads all the romance novels, so I know these things. And I see the way he looks at you when your back is turned, when you can't see him."

I wish she hadn't said that. It was like being hurt all over again.

It wasn't Mark at my door. Standing out in the snow were two police officers, a man and a woman. With their similar bowl-cut dark hair, they looked like brother and sister. I couldn't help it. I thought of Mark and Thea.

I looked from one to the other. "Yes?" I asked.

"Are you Mrs. Roarke?" asked the female.

"I am."

"We will need you to come with us."

"Come with you where?"

"To the police station."

"I, um..." I put a hand to my head. "What's this about?"

The woman introduced herself as Sally and her partner as Pete.

"What is this about?" I asked again.

"We need you to come in and answer a few questions," Pete said. The only thing I could think of was that this had something to do with the now-reopened case of Tracy York, so I asked them if this was it. They looked at each other and Sally said, "No, it isn't."

I ran a hand through my mussed hair. I said, "Can't you come in and tell me what this is about?" And then a horrific thought. *Maddy!* I gasped. "Is it Maddy? Is this about my daughter? Is she okay? Has something happened to her?" The woman smiled, touched my shivery arm and said, "Oh, no. This is about something else entirely." She seemed gentle.

"Can't you just tell me what this is about?" I pleaded.

I opened the door wide and they entered and followed me into the kitchen where we sat down at my table. I was conscious of the messiness of the place, my pots all over the floor and dirty rags draped in the sink. Close up, I could see that the two officers looked nothing alike. The woman was a good ten years older than the man. And while her hair was almost blue-black and shiny and layered up against her cheek, his was wispy and dull. His features were tiny and deep-set, while the woman was louder and big-featured and seemed friendlier. She seemed to be doing all the talking.

He took out a notebook and she said, "Okay, then. Can you confirm the fact that you were at Eloise Fremont's apartment on Thursday morning?"

I nodded and began to relax. What had I done, parked in the wrong slot? Had I fender bended a BMW on my way out? I groaned. Oh, great. That was it, wasn't it? I couldn't afford my insurance as it was!

"She's dead," the woman said.

"Excuse me?"

"She's dead and according to the doorman you were the last person in her apartment. You may have been the last person to see her alive."

"I was there on Thursday," I said.

"Her body was discovered late last night."

I counted the days on my fingers. "How horrible," I said.

"Her son had been calling her at various times throughout the weekend. Finally, late last night he went over there. The coroner is giving the time of death as sometime Thursday afternoon."

I stared at them and my mouth went dry. "She was fine when I left her. How did she die? Was it a heart attack?"

"We're not sure," Pete said. "The preliminary reports may indicate some sort of poisoning or perhaps a drug overdose."

"I didn't see anyone," I offered. "I don't know how I can be of help."

"We're going to need you to go over the entire afternoon with us," said the woman, taking out her own small notebook.

"You said she was poisoned. Did you check the tea?" I asked the police officers. "We had tea."

"It wasn't the tea," she said. "The mugs on the table are being examined now, but it appears there wasn't any poison residue. They may find something on closer examination."

The officers stayed for another hour and I had to go over my story three or four more times. At one point, he tapped his pen on his notebook and said, "We spoke with Larry. We know what happened when you were younger and the accusations your family made against the Fremonts."

I swallowed. So that was it. I was somehow being blamed? "That was a long time ago and has nothing to do with all this." But even as I said it I wondered. It was all coming over me in waves. Tracy. Mark. His business.

Thea. Paul Ashton. And what was the common denominator in everything? Larry Fremont. But still, I couldn't imagine even Larry murdering his own mother.

In the end I didn't have to go to the police station. Maybe I look too pathetic and honest, but before they left the woman pressed her business card into my hand. "Please call me if you need to talk about anything. And please call me Sally."

"I will." I promised.

Alone in my kitchen, I just sat there for a few minutes. Then I decided on coffee, but my hands shook as I poured a cup. It was bitter and cold. I poured it out and made more. Fresh coffee in hand, I called Jolene. She was horrified. I called my parents, told them everything. Right now I needed people on my side. My mother told me to be careful, but her voice was tentative. She sounded afraid herself. My father said he golfed regularly with a lawyer. He'd talk to him, get some advice.

"I don't think I'll need that," I said.

"Nevertheless, it never hurts to be prepared," she said.

My mother said, "We worry about you."

The tone of my mother's voice was almost one of resignation. It was as if she always knew something like this would happen, and now it had.

When I hung up, I cranked my music up high and cleaned out more cupboards. I worked fast, furiously. And as I did so, I tried to keep at bay certain thoughts, like…like…what if all this time I'd been wrong? What if the Fremonts were right and I hadn't seen Larry push Tracy off the bridge?

No! I dropped a pot lid and it clattered to the floor. That doesn't explain Larry's laugh! It just doesn't! Even if Tracy took her own life, that still doesn't explain the laugh. But maybe things weren't as they seemed. Look at me. I was so sure that I had left my diary and locket on my bedside table. And obviously I hadn't. Maybe I was like the reports said, crazy, loony, unstable.

Can the mind play tricks like that? Could I have imagined Larry's laugh?

And what did any of this have to do with Paul Ashton? I leaned back on my heels and closed my eyes. And it wasn't too far to go from that position to one of being on my knees. And before I knew it, I was crying and praying old forgotten prayers.

I need some help, I said I can't live like this anymore, with this fear and hatred welling up in me. I hear Tracy's screams every night when I can't sleep. I hear Larry's laugh. And then there's everything that happened in my marriage. And Maddy and her deafness. I've been angry and bitter, and I don't know what to do with this. No matter what I do it won't go away. And now this thing with Mark—it's just unfair. He's the first guy I've allowed myself to feel anything for in a long time and he was just using me…

I was cross-legged on my kitchen floor and bent forward as far as I could go, my face practically touching the floor. I stayed that way for a long time. Finally, the cold floor pressing against my cheek sent chills down my spine. I rose, slowly unwinding my body. In a very odd sort of way, a way I couldn't even define or name, I felt better. And somehow I began thinking again about forgiveness. Maybe in a weird way I was supposed to forgive all the people who had wronged me, but I needed to forgive myself first.

I went into my bathroom, blew my nose and washed my face. The phone rang.

"Ally!"

I gripped the phone. It was Mark.

"I need to see you. We didn't say good-bye on good terms, and I really don't know why. I've been thinking about it, praying about it. Can we talk? Can we meet?"

"Eloise Fremont is dead."

That stopped him. "What?"

"She was murdered. Maybe. I was the last person to see her alive. The police were just here."

Mark said, "I can't believe it."

"It's true. She's dead."

"Maybe I can help. I'll phone Thea."

"Thea," I said drily. If he picked up anything in my tone he didn't say.

Forgiveness? I was supposed to forgive her, too?

"I have to go, Mark. But I have to tell you something."

"What's that?"

"I don't swoon. I never swooned over you, nor will I ever swoon in the future over you. I am not a swooning person."

"Ally?"

I gently laid down the receiver. I expected him to call right back and he did. I didn't answer. So much for my new plan of forgiveness.

Maddy hadn't taken my diary or locket to school with her, even by accident. When she got home I asked her about it, and we went through her school bag. She helped me look all over the house and we couldn't find any trace of either. I went scrounging through my cold basement again. Maybe I had put everything back there. I hadn't.

I remember thinking about taking the diary to Sydney with me, but then decided against it. Had someone come into my house and stolen these things? And more importantly, why? My house showed no signs of being broken into. I checked all the windows.

I made supper and paid attention while Maddy told me about her day at school. After she had gone to bed, I made myself a pot of tea and stared at it while I turned on the news. There was something about tea that nagged at my memory. I couldn't place what it was.

The murder of Eloise Fremont was the top story. I watched a clip of the Fremont clan, the teary and red-faced Larry with Belle, who according to the news report had flown home from a Manhattan shopping trip to be with her husband. Larry said to the camera, "We are deeply distressed by this. My family and I are offering a fifty-thousand-dollar reward for any information leading to the arrest of the person who did this to my…my mother."

He was a good actor. His tears even looked genuine. Standing beside him, Belle looked pale and fearful.

Larry was tearfully telling the cameras that this latest murder coming so quickly on the heels of the death of his dear friend, Paul Ashton, had devastated the family. He was going to personally see to it that the entire force of the law would be brought to bear on the person or persons who had perpetrated this horrible crime.

He turned and he and Belle made their way to a waiting limo. Cameras followed them. I leaned forward.

Larry put his hand up to ward off the cameras. He said, "Can you leave us alone, please? This is a difficult time for my family and me. Can we get past, please?"

My full attention was on Belle. I squinted at the television. No, it couldn't be. Her bruise appeared to be—gone? I stared at the place on her neck where the bruise had been. Either she had healed remarkably quickly or she was an expert with concealer makeup. She pulled her scarf up to round her neck. I squinted. Then gasped. It was the same blue scarf she had worn when she'd been to my house. It was the same scarf I'd seen draped on a chair at Eloise's apartment.

When he found his mother's body, Larry could have recognized the scarf as his wife's and picked it up. Maybe the explanation was that simple.

When the news moved on to another item, I took a sip of my tea and then looked down into my teacup, puzzled. It clattered against the saucer when I set it down which jarred something inside of me. But I still couldn't remember.

In the middle of the night I woke with a jolt, realizing what it was. Mugs! The police officers had used the word mugs. *They'd checked the mugs and they were clean.*

But Eloise had poured tea into two delicate china cups. No one would refer to those teacups as mugs.

I stared at the ceiling, trying to make sense of things. I heard a noise. Downstairs? Outside? I craned to listen. It was just the snow falling off my roof. Nevertheless, I got up, made my way down the hall. I peered in at Maddy. She was sleeping soundly. I went in and pulled the blanket to her chin. Her room seemed chilly. There seemed to be a draft. It was so cold it seemed to be coming right through the walls. I turned up her heat a bit.

I went back to bed, but barely slept. When I did, I dreamed about teacups and snow. In one horrific dream I was cold and buried in the snow outside on my sundeck and couldn't claw my way free. Through all of my dreams I kept hearing Larry laugh.

I awoke to find my face smothered in my white sheet, my blankets tossed off me. I'm usually not this spooked. For almost nine years I've had to be strong for Maddy.

I don't allow myself these kind of lapses, these bad dreams, but every once in a while…

In the morning I went down to my kitchen. It was quiet in the house, which was unusual. Maddy is normally up way before me. I went and stood beside my front picture window. Footprints were barely visible in the skiff of snow on my walkway. I stared at them, wondering who could have made them. Probably anybody, I thought, from a travelling salesperson to the paperboy to someone with a political flyer. I went to my front door and in my mailbox was a manila envelope with my name printed on it in bold, black letters.

Curious, I brought it inside and opened it while I flicked on the coffeemaker. I pulled out a five-by-seven color photograph of…Maddy. I stared down at it for several seconds before realization dawned. The picture had been taken in front of her school and my daughter was laughing and kneeling in the snow. It was grainy as if taken from a great distance with a telephoto lens. She clearly didn't know she was being photographed.

My whole body trembling, I turned over the photo. A label had been affixed to the back and on it was printed, "You have a beautiful daughter."

I trembled. I made my way stumbling into the living room. Someone had done this. Gone to her school. Taken a picture of her. I panicked. Maddy! She was usually awake by now. She was *always* up before me. I tore through the living room, raced up the stairs my heart pounding. "Maddy!" I called. The draft! The window! Why hadn't I checked the window last night when I'd gone into Maddy's room? I had merely turned up the heat.

I got to her room. "Maddy! Maddy!"

I raced over to her bed.

She was there!

I slumped to my knees beside her bed. *Thank You, God!* She looked up at me through sleepy eyes. I reached for her and hugged her close for a long time. I could not stop crying. I could not stop shaking. Larry had no right to do this to me. He would pay. I would make sure he paid. I would prove that he was responsible for all of this. For Tracy. For Paul. For his mother. For Maddy. I remembered what I'd promised to my mother, that I would prove that Larry was a killer.

I could feel Maddy shrugging away from me slightly, and then she tapped my shoulder, which was our signal that she wanted to tell me something.

I backed away and signed, "What is it, pumpkin pie? Are you okay?"

"You're squeezing me too tight," she said. She giggled and fell into my arms.

FIFTEEN

Downstairs, all doors and windows checked and locked, I kept Maddy close beside me and scrambled until I found the business card that the female officer had given to me. Sally. I remembered her name. I called the number on the card, barely getting my fingers to hit the keys correctly. She answered. I couldn't get my words to come out. "Someone's threatening me," I said. "They took a picture of my daughter. Right at her school. In my mailbox. This morning. Someone. Wants to kill me." My words kept coming out in breathless spurts. "They were china teacups. Not mugs. No, they were not mugs."

"Ally? We'll send someone right over. Are you in danger now? Is someone there now?"

"No," I breathed. "They weren't in my house. They just dropped it off in the mailbox."

"Did you see anyone?"

"It was Larry. It had to be Larry. I heard something in the night. That might have been it."

"Did you see Larry?"

"No, but I know it was him. There are footprints in the snow."

"Footprints? Good. Great, in fact. Don't shovel."

"Don't worry, I won't, but it's windy," I said. "The snow is blowing."

"We'll be right there. You stay put, Ally. And make sure your doors and windows are locked. Stay close to Maddy."

"I already am." The fact was, I wasn't letting her out of my arms.

I called Jolene next and spilled out my entire story in panting sobs.

I called my parents. They asked how they could help.

A few minutes later two officers arrived and began taking pictures of my sidewalk. They came in, took a look at the picture, studied it this way and that, put it in a bag. While I was in the middle of answering their questions, Sally arrived. She put her hand on mine and asked if I was okay. I nodded numbly, then I said, "My diary is gone. The one from when I was a kid. And we had our tea in little china cups, not mugs. And the locket is missing. It was with my diary."

Sally kept her hand on mine. "Ally," she said looking into my eyes. "Can you start from the beginning?"

"Mommy?" Maddy signed. "Can I go get dressed?"

I said, "Can we go upstairs? I know it's crazy, but I just can't let her out of my sight."

"I'll walk with you," Sally said. We made our way up the stairs.

I said, "I'm keeping her home from school today."

"That's probably wise."

When we were in Maddy's room and she was getting dressed, I went through the whole story. As I got to the part about the tea, she said, "I don't remember a tea pot being at the crime scene. The report stated that two pottery coffee mugs were on the table and appeared to be rinsed out." She pulled out her cell phone and talked to someone at the station.

"Larry went right to my daughter's school and took the picture."

"Is there a safe place you can take your daughter? A friend, perhaps? Your parents'?"

"I'll call my parents again. She could go to PEI with them."

The three of us went back down to my kitchen, where Sally poured me a cup of my own coffee and set it down in front of me. Maddy got out a coloring book and crayons and sat down on the floor to work while Sally and I continued our conversation. She was writing it all down.

"Do you know how Eloise died?" I asked.

"We're still working on that."

"Was she poisoned?"

"We're still working on that."

I shook my head. "I don't think Larry meant to kill his mother. I think it was an accident. I have this idea. He meant to kill me. He knew his mother never drank tea, and he saw me drinking tea at the funeral. But I didn't drink any of Eloise's tea."

"What I can tell you is this," Sally said leaning forward and putting her folded hands on the table. "The person who killed Eloise was probably not Larry."

I nodded. "But did you look for fingerprints?" Although as I said it I realized that of course his prints would be all over the place anyway. As family, he would be there on a regular basis.

"It's not Larry. I can tell you that definitely."

"How can you be so sure?"

She shook her head and looked at her hands. "We found traces of talcum powder, the kind you get off rubber gloves. We found those gloves in a dumpster behind the condo. What people don't realize is that you can get fingerprints from the inside of gloves. But, Ally, the prints we have don't match Larry's."

"Then whose are they?"

"We're working on that."

"But they must belong to someone!"

She said again, "We're working on that."

When they left, after going over everything a dozen times more, and assuring me that they would keep watch on my house, I looked up and sitting across from me at my own table was—Mark.

I gulped when I saw him. "What are you doing here?"

"Jolene called me. She told me someone was threatening you."

"You shouldn't have come."

He said, "I wanted to. I'm worried about you. Are you okay?"

"I'm fine. You don't need to be here."

"I do." He looked at me, I felt awkward under his gaze. I didn't know what to say. He added, "I need to apologize, if nothing else. Your 'swooning' reference. I went over and over that. You heard Thea and I talking, didn't you?"

I looked over at Maddy sitting on the floor coloring in her book. She wasn't paying attention.

He said, "I haven't been totally honest with you."

I met his gaze square on. "Ya think?"

"I need to tell you everything."

"I'm not even sure I want to hear. You used me. I heard enough."

He shook his head. "It wasn't like that. Maybe that's how it started, but it didn't end up that way." He was tapping his fingers on the table nervously. "Because then I met you. Got to know you. You're nothing like what I expected."

"So meeting me was all a setup?"

"It may have started off that way, but—"

"You were hoping I'd have some dirt on Larry that you could use in your own revenge."

"That's how it started..." He was looking at me helplessly. I did not feel sorry for him.

"Your little boat design business?" I retorted. "How come Thea's so involved? Just looking out for her favorite cousin?"

"That's not what happened."

I shook my head, put my hands up. "Can you please tell me what Larry did to you? He took money from a business that you and he were starting up? Is that what this is about?"

He shook his head. "It wasn't that."

"But I thought Larry..."

He hesitated before he answered. "It wasn't just Larry. It was the Fremonts and it wasn't what they did to me personally. It was what they did to my mother's family. What they did was basically steal the coal mine out from under us."

My voice was quiet when I said, "Coal mine? I thought it was a boat design business."

"I never said what the Fremonts did to me. I let you assume, but I never said."

I stared at him. "So you lie by omission."

He frowned and looked down at his hands which were now stilled. "I owe you a big apology."

"You already said that, so apologize then."

"I'm sorry." He blinked several times.

"What did Larry do to you?" I whispered. "What kind of information were you hoping to get from me?"

He sighed and began. "The reason it's so hard is that it happened to my uncle, Thea's father. Which is why

Thea gets a little nuts about it. The Fremonts essentially bought him out. He ended up losing everything. Everything except the house. Thea's house."

He paused before continuing.

"My uncle was what you would call in today's world, bipolar, but a lot of people just called him crazy. He had highs and lows. In his high periods he was a phenomenal entrepreneur, working eighteen-hour days, thriving on little more than coffee and a bowl of cereal. When he was up, he would make deals all over the world. He knew Larry Fremont's father. But then in his low periods, everything went to pot. It was during one of his low periods that he decided to sign everything over to the Fremonts. I don't know what they did, what they promised him, but that's what he ended up doing."

I said, "But wouldn't your family have legal recourse?"

Mark shook his head. "What we did have, the Fremont lawyer tore to shreds anyway. It was all very, very legal. Eloise and Larry Fremont had this great plan, all worked out on paper, and apparently with proven documentation. Now, that coal was beginning to fail, the Fremonts were turning their attention toward gold. Their idea basically involved mine owners investing in the Fremonts' grand gold mine scheme. They had documents, according to my uncle, that proved that gold could be easily mined and was there in abundance."

I smiled. I couldn't help myself. Nova Scotia has a rich folkloric history of gold mines and hidden gold treasures. I mentioned this.

Mark's mouth formed a thin, grim line. "And my unstable uncle fell for it."

"No one else in your family had power of attorney?"

He shook his head. "You would have to have known my uncle. He refused to take medication. He didn't feel anything was wrong with him. No, he had controlled the mining interests for all these years and had done very well, and there was no reason why now, he couldn't be trusted."

"When did this happen?"

"Around ten years ago. My uncle died shortly after it happened. It was a car accident, but there is speculation that he killed himself by driving into a bridge abutment."

I looked at him. Sometimes I think I have the corner on life's sadness and then I hear other stories and I realize how untrue that is. "I'm so sorry," I said.

He went on. "I think Thea went into the police force for just this reason, to enact revenge, to bring down the Fremonts. When my cousin became a cop she did extensive research on the Fremonts. Thea researched you. She knew all about you and what happened on the bridge. She knew who you were. And she convinced me to apply for the job and work with you. I tried to convince her that I wouldn't be a party to that. But I did apply for a job and then I saw you."

I looked outside of my kitchen window to the trees, still covered in snow, and thought about what he was saying.

I said, "That still doesn't justify what you did, pretending to like me, befriending me." *Forgiveness.* The thought careened around in my brain.

He continued. "I especially didn't want to befriend you because of what happened to me four years ago."

"What was that?" I put my hands around my coffee mug, looked into the depths of it and waited.

"I went back to church. I'd been absent for a lot of years."

"Like me."

"Maybe. I guess with me I just couldn't live with this hatred of the Fremonts any longer. I needed some closure, some forgiveness. I went back to church and began a long journey back to God. With me it's been a series of ups and downs."

"Long journey…" Had I started on this long journey? I remember how I prayed on this very floor for answers from God. Is this how a long journey begins? Not with sudden revelations, but with small steps in fits and starts, one step back and then two steps forward?

"So," he was continuing. "Befriending you to get information about Larry Fremont may have been my motive at the beginning, but I have to say I'm not sorry I did."

I traced my finger around the rim of my coffee cup and said, "It must have been a shock when Paul Ashton died."

He nodded. "A great shock! Thea was hoping that Paul would share some information about Larry with her. She broached the subject in a roundabout way with him once and he shot her down. He would be no part of any scheme to discredit Larry. Paul had the mistaken impression that Larry was on the up and up."

"But my daughter." My voice was barely above a whisper when I said, "Thea used my daughter. I don't think I will ever be able to forgive her for that. Or you."

He shook his head. "Thea genuinely likes you and Maddy. If you had stayed to listen to the rest of our misbegotten conversation you would've heard Thea wondering aloud if she had done the right thing, making you go back to the bridge that afternoon. She told me she thinks your daughter is special. And no matter how much I've tried to talk her out of it, I guess she wants revenge more than any kind of forgiveness." Then he said quietly, so quietly that I barely heard, "Larry has called me a few times over the past couple of months. In one of the messages he said he wanted to make things right. Those were his words. *Make things right.* I never called him back. I don't know what he wants."

I nodded without saying anything.

We were quiet for a while after that. Then he said, "I've told you that I'm sorry, and truly I am. I would like to know that you forgive me."

I looked away. "I don't know if I can do that." I glanced over at Maddy who was walking her ponies along the floor next to the wall. "I just don't know."

SIXTEEN

My parents drove over that evening. They didn't know the particulars. All they knew was that I was being threatened, and that it had something to do with the Fremonts. They had been planning to go to Quebec City on a shopping trip. Now they would take Maddy. I called the school and said she was going on a trip with her grandparents for a few days.

On the day the three of them left, my mother followed me upstairs to get Maddy's things. "What's this about?" She wanted to know.

I told her I was being stalked by Larry Fremont, that he was threatening me.

"I told you to be careful. I warned you to leave things alone," said my mother folding a shirt of Maddy's on her lap.

So it's my fault? I wanted to scream. Because I didn't leave things alone? I didn't say that however.

Maddy came upstairs with my father and I helped her pack Curly Duck and three of her ponies. More negotiating. Maddy wanted to take a dozen. I said three. How about seven? Three.

Her grandfather said, "Let her take a dozen. We have room."

When they drove away the sun shone down and I hugged her tightly and signed, "Good-bye, pumpkin pie. Be a good girl for Grandma and Grandpa." Then I hugged her again. On the corner, across the street was a police car.

As soon as they left, I changed my mind, wanted to call her back. How could I be sure she would be safe even with them? What if Larry was following them? What if he knew where they were going?

Jolene came over in the evening to be with me. I knew it was to keep my mind off everything, but she paraded in front of me.

"Notice anything different?"

I didn't.

"The baby has dropped. My doctor is telling me that she could be born at any moment."

She pirouetted around me, which got me laughing. Only Jolene would have so much energy moments before giving birth. I was practically on the couch entire weeks before Maddy was born.

"I do have a bone to pick with you, however," I said.

"And what bone would that be?" She said sitting down and tucking her legs underneath her.

"You called Mark."

"Did I or did I not do a good thing by calling Mark?"

"That's not the point."

"It is the point. Rod and I know Mark. He's honest and would never hurt anyone. I knew there had to be a misunderstanding and you see? There was. When are you seeing him again?"

I shrugged. I didn't know. In a little while she was scrounging my kitchen for canned goods. "I'm making you some soup," she said.

"Don't you have to get home to Rod?"

"He knows I'm here. He knows I need to be here. You can't be alone tonight. My mother is keeping him company."

"Thank you, Jolene."

"Just one thing, though. If this baby starts popping, you have to promise to drive me to the hospital and call Rod."

Later when the two of us were comfortably watching the news, there were Larry and Belle again in the clip they kept showing over and over. The way she shrugged away from Larry's grasp as they get into the waiting limo. The way she pulled the blue scarf up around her neck.

As I watched an edge of an idea began percolating in my brain. I was thinking about Belle. I was remembering a tall, proud girl who was raised by a single father who worked the mines to support her and the brood of little brothers. I was remembering a girl who saw marrying into the Fremont clan as a way of escape. I was thinking about the way she clung to Larry at Paul's funeral, the way he patted her hand like a father would a child's, and not the way a husband would touch his wife.

It looked as if Belle was shrugging away from Larry, but what if it was the other way around? Was my blindness to anything good about Larry causing me to see things not the way they were but the way I wanted them to be?

The news flicked to another item, and then another, I couldn't concentrate.

"Look at that." Jolene was laughing. The news had moved to a light item about a monkey escaping from the zoo and how animal control had rescued him from where he'd climbed high up in the tree.

"A tree!" I said excitedly and pointed.

"Yes. A tree." She looked at me sideways. "A monkey in a tree."

"That's it!" I said. "The tree!"

"Excuse me?"

"Zacchaeus was in a tree."

"Who?"

"Zacchaeus. From the Bible. Do you remember that Bible story?"

"My dear," she said patting my knee. "I have even less Bible schooling than you do. I never heard of Zacchaeus."

"Okay." I got up and began wandering around my house. "I've got to have a Bible around here."

I kept remembering what Carolyn had said a week ago about Larry's Zacchaeus Plan. I sat down in front of my computer and looked up Zacchaeus on the Internet. One Web site told the story of the little man who climbed up into a sycamore tree to see Jesus, but that wasn't all. He was also the shrewd businessman who decided to give half of his money to the poor and pay back four times everyone he had wronged.

I blinked.

Larry had called Mark about wanting to "make things right." I thought about it. There was something here. I thought about it after Jolene left. I thought about it as I made my way to bed. I thought about it all night. I dreamed about it.

At about eight-thirty the following morning I went outside and talked to the officers in the police car. I laid everything out for them. All of it. Then I came back inside.

I called the Fremont house. Belle answered the phone and I asked if I could meet with her, maybe come to her house to see her. I needed to talk with her. She sounded upbeat, happy to hear me.

"Larry's here, but he's in the shower."

"I don't need to see Larry. Just you, Belle."

An hour later I was standing in front of the massive Fremont front door and ringing the decorative door chime.

Belle answered the door herself. "Hello, Alicia," she said calmly and opened it wide. I entered just as calmly. She was dressed all in black and barefoot. She wore no makeup and the bruise on her chin, I noticed, had miraculously disappeared. Surprise. Surprise. Her eyes seemed bright, too bright. I became alarmed, just a little.

"Why don't you come into my house? I have tea."

Tea. Right.

I followed her. There was none of the tentativeness she had displayed at my house when she told me to leave this whole thing alone. There was none of the nervous touching of her face, bringing her scarf up to hide the bruise. This was Belle's house and she was in control.

I followed her down an enormous hall to a breakfast nook in the back of the house. As I did so, I realized that she had gotten what she had wanted all of her life: rich husband, fancy house, all the money she could possibly want. But it wasn't enough. It never is. Nothing is ever enough when there is that gnawing place inside of you that demands more and more and more and is never filled.

"I'm glad you came," she said sitting down on a stool and wrapping her long legs around it. "I wasn't sure you would, you know. I wanted to talk to you again."

She swiveled from side to side on the stool while she regarded me cocking her head from side to side. I remained standing.

"Larry's not here, is he?" I asked.

"Nope." She grinned. "It's just you and me."

I nodded.

She said, "I told you to stay out of it, Alicia. But you wouldn't. Even when we were girls you wouldn't."

"It was you," I said, "Who called Tracy's father and pretended to be me."

She grinned. "You're so perceptive. I told him that Tracy was seducing Larry. I'm not sure I used that exact expression, maybe I said she was 'coming on to him' or something. I suggested that it was even serious enough to affect his employment with the mine."

"So you could end up with Larry. Even at sixteen you had your sights set on Larry."

She shrugged and swiveled in her chair. "Stupid man," she said. "Now, suddenly, he has this great plan to give away all his money, to everyone he had 'wronged,' is how he puts it."

The Zacchaeus Plan, I thought.

She went on. "...To charity and poor people." She spat out the last word. I reflected that she had once been poor. I wondered if she even remembered that.

"You're crazy," I muttered.

She lifted her eyebrows theatrically. "Not me. You're the crazy one. You're the one who told all those lies about Larry way back when Tracy died, and you're still the crazy one now. Still believing that old lie. I have your diary and locket by the way."

"I know. I figured it out last night. My spare key is missing."

"That was me, of course. When I excused myself to go to the bathroom I looked for a spare key. Everyone has one and they usually keep them in very obvious places, like hanging on a hook right next to the back door."

"Why did you want my diary?"

"The story. I had to know exactly what you thought happened with Tracy."

"Why now, after all this time?"

"You'd teamed up with Mark. I had to know what you

knew. I couldn't have Larry giving away all my money. That was my money. He has no right to give it all away."

I said, "I notice that the bruise on your chin has miraculously healed. Was that bruise to make me feel sorry for you? To make me think Larry was a bad guy?"

"That is MY money!" Her eyes were like fire. And for the first time I began to be afraid. This was a woman who'd killed at least twice. Why did I think I was immune? She rubbed her chin and added, "There's a lot you can do with stage makeup." She paused and said, "Stupid man. Got religion. I couldn't..." She looked away and bit her lip. "I couldn't lose everything I'd worked so hard for."

I took a breath and said, "Did you mean for me to die, too? When Eloise died? I imagine you were pretty surprised when I showed up alive."

She looked at me, flicked her hair off her shoulder and nodded. "Stupid woman drinks only coffee. No, that rat poison in the tea was meant for you."

She leaned forward and for one horrid moment I thought she was going to jump up from the stool, pick up the nearest heavy object and whack me over the head with it. Like she had done with Paul Ashton.

"You killed Ashton," I stammered.

"That was easy. After Larry became a born-again Christian..." She sing-songed the words. "He hired Paul to help him liquidate many of his assets. It wouldn't be long before he realized that I was taking a lot of Larry's money, squirreling it away. I couldn't have that now, could I?"

I was casting back. "What about the boat contract, the one that Rod and I lost. That was your doing, wasn't it?" I remembered what she said when she showed up at my house late at night.

They can make contracts disappear.

She laughed out loud now. It was a mirthless sound. "Now you are giving me too much credit. Even I couldn't pull off something like that!"

She flicked her head back. I noticed for the first time how dull her hair was. It looked unwashed, slightly oily. There was something off about her. I wondered how many days she'd gone without a shower.

"No, that was simply a happy coincidence. I did, however, alert my friend in California who works in a big boat-building company about the bid."

I stared at her.

"I could kill you now," she said. "But I know my chances. I'm not stupid. Third time would definitely be unlucky for me. So you're safe. You can breathe easy for the time being. Instead, I'm going to control you from now on."

"What do you mean?" I asked a little bit incredulously.

"Little Maddy." She leered. "I know where she is. I know she's in Quebec City with her grandparents. I happen to know the hotel they're in, let's see, the Motel le Voyageur. You want to know the room number? I have that, too."

I wanted to kill her right then. I wanted to reach across the room and put my hands around her neck and strangle her. Instead, I took a deep breath and looked at her. "How dare you!" I said.

"I know where she goes to school." Very quietly she whispered. "Of course, you know that I know that. You got the picture. That's why you're here. That picture was meant as a warning. You will butt out now. And if I see or hear of you meddling in my affairs, something will happen to Maddy. Don't forget it."

The finality of that whisper terrified me.

I stared at her, dumfounded, terrified and not knowing what to do. I glanced at the door.

"I hope Maddy has a good time with her grandparents," Belle said. "And you know, she has to come back to Halifax some time." Her gaze was stone. "You can go now. But remember, I know. I know what you love more than anything. You will stay out of my business. I have the upper hand."

I left then. But as I closed her door behind me I gave her one long last look. She didn't know it, but it wasn't she who had the upper hand. It was me.

SEVENTEEN

As soon as I walked out of Belle's house and shut the door behind me, two police officers entered without knocking to arrest her. Sally came over, put her hand on my shoulder and told me what a great job I'd done. Sally, plus a whole raft of cops, had been monitoring everything that had gone on in the house via a transmitter and microphone attached to an inside pocket of my jacket.

I climbed into the van, sat on a seat and put my head in my hands. I felt as if I would collapse.

"You did great," said one of the officers patting my shoulder.

Someone handed me a large coffee. I practically drank it down in one gulp. From the van window I could see Belle being led away in handcuffs. I began shaking when I saw her. It was all over now. There were so many ways that it could have gone wrong, yet I knew it had to be me who went in there. That Belle would open up only to me.

In fact, my daughter wasn't in the Motel le Voyageur in Quebec City. That had been a ruse. My parents had been stopped somewhere along the TransCanada by the RCMP who had taken them all to a safe place in Fredericton, New Brunswick. I would be seeing her tonight.

And now as I sat trembling in the back of the police

van, holding my coffee cup, I closed my eyes. When I opened them, Larry was there. He'd been there all along, sitting in the back of the van. His face was ashen.

"Thank you for what you did," he added barely above a whisper.

I didn't say anything. Here was the man I'd hated, feared, most of my life. And he was thanking me.

"My wife..." he stammered. He bowed his head before he went on. He took a breath and continued. "When I saw you and Mark at the funeral, I realized that I had chosen the right path. To make things right. To get going on my Zacchaeus Plan. It's what I hired Paul for. I think I knew right from the beginning that Belle had...that Belle was somehow involved in Paul's death. I just didn't want to admit it—couldn't admit it to myself. My mother supported my plan."

I played with the edge of my cardboard coffee cup.

He went on. "She didn't share my desire to do what I needed to do, but she respected me. I met Paul last summer. Golfing. He made such an impression on me. We had lots of talks. I became a Christian. I didn't want a lot of fanfare. Everything I have ever done in my life has been accompanied by too much fanfare. I decided I wanted this to be quiet. I know what I've been, what I've done. I wanted to make it up."

I was shredding bits of the paper cup in my hand. I looked at him and said, "But what about Tracy? You still have to pay for what you did to her. How will you repay that? Are you going to jail, then? Are you giving yourself up?"

He sighed deeply, looked down at his hands on his knees. "I know you don't believe this, but I didn't push Tracy. We were arguing. She said she was going to jump off if I didn't leave Belle for her. I told her no, that

I was in love with Belle…" He choked on those words. "Such a long time ago…" He paused. "We were all just kids…" No one said anything for a few minutes. Even the police officers who were sitting in the van said nothing. "I didn't kill her, Alicia. I know what you think you saw, but I was trying to hold her back."

"No." I forced myself to look into his eyes. "You laughed. I have heard that laugh in every nightmare I have ever had."

He nodded slowly. "I did laugh. I'm not quite sure why. I was young and stupid, and I thought she would land in the water and swim away. My laugh has haunted me all my life, too. I think it was my laugh that finally brought me to God."

EPILOGUE

Maddy was home. Safe. And this whole thing was over. So I should be happy. I should be relieved. Well, I was relieved but not necessarily happy. I was mostly exhausted. Maddy and I had fallen asleep watching a movie on television. I think she was as tired as I was. My parents were still here visiting, and happened to be out now, grocery shopping for the four of us.

I hadn't seen Mark since the evening when I told him I wasn't sure I could forgive him. I'd been doing a lot of thinking since then. Because I realized something. I was no different than Mark. I knew well the fierce anger a person could hold. Revenge and fear had colored my life for so many years, and given half a chance, wouldn't I have done exactly what Mark and Thea had?

When that realization hit, I could do nothing but pray. I held a sleeping Maddy on my lap and said, "God, please forgive me. I need to begin this long journey…"

I stopped praying and sat quietly for a moment. Maybe God hadn't caused all the bad things that had ever happened to me. *God is love.* How many times had I heard that in my childhood? He was just as sad as I was when Tracy died, when Sterling walked out on me, when Maddy was born deaf. I began to understand something then—God didn't cause these things to happen, but through these bad things, I could learn to love God. And also learn to trust Him.

I knew as I sat there, gently stroking Maddy's hair, that I needed to forgive the Fremonts. I needed to forgive Larry. I needed to forgive Sterling. If not for their sakes, then for mine.

For so long—too long—my back had been turned away from God. I was ready now to turn around and face Him.

I sat up. It was the doorbell. I got up slowly, extricating myself from Maddy without waking her. Maybe it was Sally with some new information. Maybe it was Rod and Jolene. If her baby wasn't born tonight, she was scheduled to go into the hospital tomorrow. I'd be there with her. I straightened my crumpled sweatshirt and yawned as I made my way toward the insistent bell. I stumbled to the door in a bit of a fog and peeked around the long window beside my door and saw—roses.

I opened the door and there stood an embarrassed-looking Mark. His jeans actually looked pressed. He wore a down vest over an Irish fisherman's sweater. I guess my mouth was pretty much open, but I did not know what to say. Mark beat me to it.

"Ally, I came because I'm sorry. I'm sorry for putting my own desire for revenge above our friendship. I've been doing a lot of praying about this. I had a long talk with Larry. He told me. You did a very brave thing. And Ally, there's so much we need to talk about, but well, my most pressing problem at the moment are these flowers. Do you have a vase or something I could put them in? They were selling them at the grocery store and I feel it's important to support the local economy." His eyes twinkled and he grinned at me.

My mouth was now closed, but my knees did not seem to want to work. I was leaning against the doorframe, needing to hold myself up.

"Would you like to come in?" I whispered. I wasn't trying to whisper, that was just how it came out. "Maybe I could find that vase."

"You're going to need more than one, I fear." The twinkle in his eyes turned into a full, five-hundred-watt grin. "I have something else," he said entering with the armload of roses. "As I have said, I like to support other local economies and I just happen to have dinner reservations for tonight. I ran into your mother and father at the grocery store and they said they wanted to take Maddy out for supper, seeing how they missed their trip to Quebec."

My eyes were starting to mist up a bit. I couldn't say anything. My voice wasn't working any better than my knees.

We went into the kitchen and put the roses in three vases. Yes, three. What Mark brought would not fit in just two. I turned at a noise and there was Maddy, jumping up and down and grinning even more than Mark, if that were possible.

"Is one vase for me?" she signed.

"I think they're for both of us, pumpkin pie," I signed to her.

"He must really like you, Mom," she signed.

"Maddy, stop," I signed.

"I like him," she signed, "Do you like him, too?"

It seemed to be really warm in here.

Mark was watching our hands going at ninety miles an hour and had a quizzical look on his face. "I've got to learn that language," he said.

"But that wouldn't be any fun," I said to him. "Then

we couldn't talk behind your back or even in front of your face."

He smiled at me and then his expression became serious. "Are you okay, Ally? You've been through a lot."

"I'm okay. I'm good."

"How about tonight? Those reservations?"

I said, "That would be nice."

"I can pick you up at seven, if that's okay?" he asked. "Have you been to Deco Halifax?"

"Mark, Deco Halifax!" I exclaimed, misting up again.

I knew about Deco Halifax. It had a dining room reminiscent of Paris in the 1920s. It was right downtown. It had seafood to die for. What would I wear? My hair was a mess. My face was a mess.

"I'd love to," I said.

Mark turned to go and stopped.

"Oh here," he said, handing me an envelope. I opened it up and pulled out a check. For fifty thousand dollars. Made out to me.

"What is this? A joke?"

"It's the reward check. I had a long meeting with Larry. He asked me to deliver it to you."

"Mark." The check felt like fire. I dropped it and it fluttered to the floor. "I don't want his money. I just don't. Not now. Not ever."

"Well, it's yours. You deserve it."

"But." I looked down at the check with my name on it and with so many zeros. On the check was written, *For information leading to the arrest of,* but my eyes had trouble focusing. More help for Maddy, credit card bills, house payments, financing for the *Maddy.*

"Oh Mark, I can't take this. I can't take their money."

I bent down to pick it up from the floor. When I rose, Mark was standing close to me, very close. He reached out and touched my cheek. I remembered when Eloise had offered me money. I had flatly refused. Wasn't this the same thing?

"Larry wants to do this. Take it. You earned it."

I looked deep into Mark's eyes and began to reflect on what I had been learning about forgiveness. This was not a bribe. This was Larry asking for forgiveness. This was Larry acting on his Zacchaeus Plan. This was also another way that God was showing His love for me, His child. Just like I showed my love for Maddy.

I put the check down on the table and put the sugar bowl on top of it.

"I'll take it," I said.

"And how about me?"

"How about you what?"

"Will you take me, too?"

I grinned and went into his waiting arms.

* * * * *

Dear Reader,

Shadows on the River is the last installment in my "Shadows" series; three women who must confront the shadows in their past before they can move on to faith in God and love in the present. When she was thirteen, Ally Roarke watched her best friend die. It was a horrific experience and something she has never forgotten. She has lived most of her life in fear, wondering why God allowed such a thing to happen. All the situations in her life—her failed marriage, her hearing-impaired daughter, her failed business attempts, her insomnia—are blamed on God and she traces them right back to that day at the river.

She is sure she will never get over what she saw. What she learns by the end is that God in His infinite love and forgiveness can erase even the most horrific of memories. She also must learn to forgive.

I think a lot of us have difficulties with forgiveness. Someone has wronged us. We are hurt and confused and hold that grudge far into the future. What we fail to realize is that it's only ourselves we hurt by our failure to forgive.

I hope you enjoy *Shadows on the River.* I would love to hear your own story of forgiveness. You can e-mail me at *Linda@writerhall.com.* I also invite you to my Web site: http://writerhall.com where you can sign up for my newsletter and read my blog.

Linda Hall

Linda Hall

QUESTIONS FOR DISCUSSION

1. Has there ever been someone in your life who wronged you so badly you just couldn't forgive him/her? What finally ended up happening?

2. Jesus told Peter to forgive "seventy times seven" (*Matthew* 18:21-22). What did he mean by that? Why is it so important to forgive?

3. Have you ever been the recipient of forgiveness? How did it make you feel?

4. Ally was haunted by the memory of what she witnessed when she was thirteen. Is there an experience in your past that you just can't forget and that colors everything in your present? What can you do about it? What did Ally do about it?

5. Which character in *Shadows on the River* did you identify with and why?

6. Belle had everything, but in the end she only wanted more. What is most important to you right now? (Be honest.)

7. Do you think Ally should've taken the check at the end? Would you have? Why or why not? What would you do with the money?

8. Ally talked about a "long journey" back to God. Do you think coming to God is a long journey or an instantaneous moment? How has it been in your life?

9. Larry kept his Zacchaeus Plan quiet. Do you think this was a wise idea? Why or why not? If you had been Larry, what would you have done?

10. Ally's parents didn't quite believe their own daughter. If you had been Ally's mother would you have believed her?

11. Thea was bent on revenge. Do you think she was justified?

12. There is a fine balance between revenge and justice. Where do you think Carolyn fit in the spectrum? Was she bent on revenge or was she seeking justice for the death of her husband? How do we walk that line in our own culture?

13. Which character in the book would you like to sit down and have a nice long chat with? What are the questions you would like to ask him or her?

Turn the page for a sneak peek of Shirlee McCoy's suspense-filled story,
THE DEFENDER'S DUTY
On sale in May 2009 from Steeple Hill Love Inspired® Suspense.

After weeks in intensive care, police officer Jude Sinclair is finally recovering from the hit-and-run accident that nearly cost him his life. But was it an accident after all? Jude has his doubts—which get stronger when he spots a familiar black car outside his house: the same kind that accelerated before running him down two months ago. Whoever wants him dead hasn't given up, and anyone close to Jude is in danger. Especially Lacey Carmichael, the stubborn, beautiful home-care aide who refuses to leave his side, even if it means following him into danger….

"We don't have time for an argument," Jude said. "Take a look outside. What do you see?"

Lacey looked and shrugged. "The parking lot."

"Can you see your car?"

"Sure. It's parked under the streetlight. Why?"

"See the car to its left?"

"Yeah. It's a black sedan." Her heart skipped a beat as she said the words, and she leaned closer to the glass. "You don't think that's the same car you saw at the house tonight, do you?"

"I don't know, but I'm going to find out."

Lacey scooped up the grilled-cheese sandwich and shoved it into the carryout bag. "Let's go."

He eyed her for a moment, his jaw set, his gaze hot. "*We're* not going anywhere. You are staying here. I am going to talk to the driver of that car."

"I think we've been down this road before and I'm pretty sure we both know where it leads."

"It leads to you getting fired. Stay put until I get back, or forget about having a place of your own for a month." He stood and limped away, not even giving Lacey a second glance as he crossed the room and headed into the diner's kitchen area.

Probably heading for a back door.

Lacey gave him a one-minute head start and then followed, the hair on the back of her neck standing on end and issuing a warning she couldn't ignore. Danger. It was somewhere close by again, and there was no way she was going to let Jude walk into it alone. If he fired her, so be it. As a matter of fact, if he fired her, it might be for the best. Jude wasn't the kind of client she was used to working for. Sure, there'd been other young men, but none of them had seemed quite as vital or alive as Jude. He didn't seem to need her, and Lacey didn't want to be where she wasn't needed. On the other hand, she'd felt absolutely certain moving to Lynchburg was what God wanted her to do.

"So, which is it, Lord? Right or wrong?" She whispered the words as she slipped into the diner's hot kitchen. A cook glared at her, but she ignored him. Until she knew for sure why God had brought her to Lynchburg, Lacey could only do what she'd been paid to do—make sure Jude was okay.

With that in mind, she crossed the room, heading for the exit and the client that she was sure was going to be a lot more trouble than she'd anticipated when she'd accepted the job.

Jude eased around the corner of the restaurant, the dark alleyway offering him perfect cover as he peered into the parking lot. The car he'd spotted through the window of the restaurant was still parked beside Lacey's. Black. Four door. Honda. It matched the one that had pulled up in front of his house, and the one that had run him down in New York.

He needed to get closer.

A soft sound came from behind him. A rustle of

fabric. A sigh of breath. Spring rain and wildflowers carried on the cold night air. Lacey.

Of course.

"I told you that you were going to be fired if you didn't stay where you were."

"Do you know how many times someone has threatened to fire me?"

"Based on what I've seen so far, a lot."

"Some of my clients fire me ten or twenty times a day."

"Then I guess I've got a ways to go." Jude reached back and grabbed her hand, pulling her up beside him.

"Is the car still there?"

"Yeah."

"Let me see." She squeezed in closer, her hair brushing his chin as she jockeyed for a better position.

Jude pulled her up short. Her wrist was warm beneath his hand. For a moment he was back in the restaurant, Lacey's creamy skin peeking out from under her dark sweater, white scars crisscrossing the tender flesh. She'd shoved her sleeve down too quickly for him to get a good look, but the glimpse he'd gotten was enough. There was a lot more to Lacey than met the eye. A lot she hid behind a quick smile and a quicker wit. She'd been hurt before, and he wouldn't let it happen again. No way was he going to drag her into danger. Not now. Not tomorrow. Not ever. As soon as they got back to the house, he was going to do exactly what he'd threatened—fire her.

"It's not the car." She said it with such authority, Jude stepped from the shadows and took a closer look.

"Why do you say that?"

"The one back at the house had tinted glass. Really dark. With this one, you can see in the back window. Looks like there is a couple sitting in the front seats.

Unless you've got two people after you, I don't think that's the same car."

She was right.

Of course she was.

Jude could see inside the car, see the couple in the front seats. If he'd been thinking with his head instead of acting on the anger that had been simmering in his gut for months, he would have seen those things long before now. "You'd make a good detective, Lacey."

"You think so? Maybe I should make a career change. Give up home-care aide for something more dangerous and exciting." She laughed as she pulled away from his hold and stepped out into the parking lot, but there was tension in her shoulders and in the air. As if she sensed the danger that had been stalking Jude, felt it as clearly as Jude did.

"I'm not sure being a detective is as dangerous or as exciting as people think. Most days it's a lot of running into brick walls. Backing up, trying a new direction." He spoke as he led Lacey across the parking lot, his body still humming with adrenaline.

"That sounds like life to me. Running into brick walls, backing up and trying new directions."

"True, but in my job the brick walls happen every other day. In life, they're usually not as frequent." He waited while she got into her car, then closed the door, glancing in the black sedan as he walked past. An elderly woman smiled and waved at him, and Jude waved back, still irritated with himself for the mistake he'd made.

Now that he was closer, it was obvious the two cars he'd seen weren't the same. The one at his place had been sleeker and a little more sporty. Which proved that when a person wanted to see something badly enough, he did.

"That wasn't much of a meal for you. Sorry to cut things short for a false alarm." He glanced at Lacey as he got into the Mustang, and was surprised that her hand was shaking as she shoved the key into the ignition.

He put a hand on her forearm. "Are you okay?"

"Fine."

"For someone who is fine, your hands sure are shaking hard."

"How about we chalk it up to fatigue?"

"How about you admit you were scared?"

"Were? I still am." She started the car, and Jude let his hand fall away from her arm.

"You don't have to be. We're safe. For now."

"It's the 'for now' part that's got me worried. Who's trying to kill you, Jude? Why?"

"If I had the answers to those questions, we wouldn't be sitting here talking about it."

"You don't even have a suspect?"

"Lacey, I've got a dozen suspects. More. Every wife who's ever watched me cart her husband off to jail. Every son who's ever seen me put handcuffs on his dad. Every family member or friend who's sat through a murder trial and watched his loved one get convicted because of the evidence I put together."

"Have you made a list?"

"I've made a hundred lists. None of them have done me any good. Until the person responsible comes calling again, I've got no evidence, no clues and no way to link anyone to the hit and run."

"Maybe he won't come calling again. Maybe the hit and run was an accident, and maybe the sedan we saw outside your house was just someone who got lost and ended up in the wrong place." She sounded like she really wanted to believe it. He should let her. That's what he'd done with his family. Let them believe the hit and run was a fluke thing that had happened and was over. He'd done it to keep them safe. He'd do the opposite to keep Lacey from getting hurt.

* * * * *

9/9

Love Inspired® SUSPENSE

TITLES AVAILABLE NEXT MONTH

Available May 12, 2009

THE DEFENDER'S DUTY by Shirlee McCoy
The Sinclair Brothers

Recuperating cop Jude Sinclair doesn't want anyone near him—especially not beautiful health aide Lacey Carmichael. His attacker *will* be back. And anyone close to him is at risk....

DEADLY COMPETITION by Roxanne Rustand
Without a Trace

The single mother is still missing, and her daughter needs more care than her uncle, Clint Herald, knows how to give. Nanny Mandy Erick steps in so capably that Clint enters her in a Mother of the Year contest. With Mandy's secrets, though, attention could be deadly.

PROTECTING HER CHILD by Debby Giusti
Magnolia Medical

Before she dies, wealthy heiress Eve Townsend must find the daughter she gave up for adoption. Medical researcher Pete Worth is ready to find answers. Instead, he uncovers more questions when he finds Meredith Lassiter widowed, pregnant—and on the run.

THE TAKING OF CARLY BRADFORD by Ramona Richards
When Dee Kelley finds a pair of child's sandals in the woods, she's determined to help find the missing girl. Nothing police chief Tyler Madison says can dissuade her. But Tyler isn't the only one who wants her off the case. And it's not just evidence awaiting Dee in the woods.

LISCNMBPA0409